Now and Forever

ALSO BY RAY BRADBURY

Ahmed and the Oblivion Machines

Bradbury Speaks

Bradbury Stories

The Cat's Pajamas

Dandelion Wine

Dark Carnival

Death Is a Lonely Business

Driving Blind

Fahrenheit 451

Farewell Summer

From the Dust Returned

A Graveyard for Lunatics

Green Shadows, White Whale

The Halloween Tree

I Sing the Body Electric!

The Illustrated Man

Let's All Kill Constance

Long After Midnight

The Machineries of Joy

The Martian Chronicles

A Medicine for Melancholy

The October Country

One More for the Road

Quicker Than the Eye

R Is for Rocket

S Is for Space

Something Wicked This Way Comes

A Sound of Thunder

The Stories of Ray Bradbury

The Toynbee Convector

When Elephants Last in the Dooryard Bloomed

Yestermorrow

Zen in the Art of Writing

Now and Forever

Somewhere a Band Is Playing
&
Leviathan '99

Ray Bradbury

HARPER LUXE
An Imprint of HarperCollinsPublishers

 For information address HarperCollins Publishers, 10 East 53rd Street, New York, NY 10022.

HarperCollins books may be purchased for educational, business, or sales promotional use. For information please write: Special Markets Department, HarperCollins Publishers, 10 East 53rd Street, New York, NY 10022.

FIRST HARPERLUXE EDITION

Library of Congress Cataloging-in-Publication is available upon request

ISBN: 978-0-06-126037-7
ISBN-10: 0-06-126037-1

07 08 09 10 11 ID/RRD 10 9 8 7 6 5 4 3 2 1

Contents

Somewhere A Band Is Playing

“Somewhere”

Some stories—be they short stories, novellas, or novels—you may realize, are written as a result of a single, immediate, clear impulse. Others ricochet off various events over a lifetime and come together much later to make a whole.

When I was six years old my father, who had an urge to travel, took our family by train to Tucson, Arizona, for a year, where we lived in a burgeoning environment; for me, it was exhilarating. The town was very small and it was still growing. There’s nothing more exciting than to be part of the evolution of a place. I felt a sense of freedom there and I made many wonderful friends.

A year later, we moved back to Waukegan, Illinois, where I had been born and spent the first years of my life. But we returned to Tucson when I was twelve, and this time I experienced an even greater sense of exhilaration because we lived out on the edge of town and I walked to school every day, through the desert, past all the fantastic varieties of cacti, encountering lizards, spiders and, on occasion, snakes, on my way to seventh grade; that was the year I began to write.

Then, much later, when I lived in Ireland for almost a year, writing the screenplay of *Moby Dick* for John Huston, I encountered the works of Stephen Leacock, the Canadian humorist. Among them was a charming little book titled *Sunshine Sketches of a Little Town.*

I was so taken with the book that I tried to get MGM to make a motion picture of it. I typed up a few preliminary pages to show the studio how I envisioned the book as a film. When MGM's interest failed, I was left with the beginning of a screenplay that had the feeling of a small town. But at the same time I couldn't help but remember the Tucson I had known and loved when I was six and when I was twelve, and began to write my own screenplay and short story about a town somewhere in the desert.

During those same years I kept encountering Katharine Hepburn, either in person or on the screen, and I was terribly attracted by the fact that she remained so youthful in appearance through the years.

Sometime in 1956, when she was in her late forties, she made the film *Summertime.* This caused me somehow to put her at the center of a story for which I had no title yet, but *Somewhere a Band Is Playing* was obviously evolving.

Some thirty years ago I saw a film called *The Wind and the Lion,* starring Sean Connery and with a fabulous score by Jerry Goldsmith. I was so taken with the score that I sat down, played it, and wrote a long poem based on the enchanting music.

This became another element of *Somewhere a Band Is Playing* as I progressed through the beginnings of a story which I had not yet fully comprehended, but it seemed as if finally all the elements were coming together: the year I spent in Tucson, age six, the year I spent there when I was twelve, the various encounters with Katharine Hepburn, including her magical appearance in *Summertime,* and my long poem based on the score of *The Wind and the Lion.* All of these ran together and inspired me to begin a long prologue to the novella that ultimately followed.

Today, looking back, I realize how fortunate I am to have collected such elements, to have held them ready, and then put them together to make this final product, *Somewhere a Band Is Playing.* I have been fortunate to have many "helpers" along the way. One of those, in the case of this story, is my dear friend Anne Hardin, who has offered me strong encouragement over the past few years to see this novella published. For that she shares in the dedication of this work.

Of course, I had hoped to finish the novella, over the years, in order to have it ready in time for Katharine Hepburn, no matter how old she got, to play the lead in a theater or film adaptation. Katie waited patiently, but the years passed, she became tired, and finally left this world. I cannot help but feel she deserves the dedication I have placed on this story.

SOMEWHERE A BAND IS PLAYING . . .

for Anne Hardin and Katharine Hepburn,
with love

Chapter 1

There was a desert prairie filled with wind and sun and sagebrush and a silence that grew sweetly up in wildflowers. There was a rail track laid across this silence and now the rail track shuddered.

Soon a dark train charged out of the east with fire and steam and thundered through the station. On its way it slowed at a platform littered with confetti, the tatters of ancient tickets punched by transient conductors.

The locomotive slowed just enough for one piece of luggage to catapult out, and a young man in a summer dishrag suit to leap after and land running as the train, with a roar, charged on as if the station did not exist, nor the luggage, nor its owner who now stopped his jolting run to stare around as the dust settled around him and, in the distance, the dim outlines of small houses were revealed.

"Damn," he whispered. "There *is* something here, after all."

More dust blew away, revealing more roofs, spires, and trees.

"Why?" he whispered. "Why did I come here?"

He answered himself even more quietly, "Because."

Chapter 2

Because.

In his half-sleep last night he had felt something writing on the insides of his eyelids.

Without opening his eyes he read the words as they scrolled:

Somewhere a band is playing,
Playing the strangest tunes,
Of sunflower seeds and sailors
Who tide with the strangest moons.
Somewhere a drummer simmers
And trembles with times forlorn,
Remembering days of summer
In futures yet unborn.

"Hold on," he heard himself say.

He opened his eyes and the writing stopped.

He half-raised his head from the pillow and then, thinking better of it, lay back down.

With his eyes closed the writing began again on the inside of his lids.

Futures so far they are ancient
And filled with Egyptian dust,
That smell of the tomb and the lilac,
And seed that is spent from lust,
And peach that is hung on a tree branch
Far out in the sky from one's reach,
There mummies as lovely as lobsters
Remember old futures and teach.

For a moment he felt his eyes tremble and shut tight, as if to change the lines or make them fade.

Then, as he watched in the darkness, they formed again in the inner twilight of his head, and the words were these:

And children sit by on the stone floor
And draw out their lives in the sands,
Remembering deaths that won't happen
In futures unseen in far lands.
Somewhere a band is playing

Where the moon never sets in the sky
And nobody sleeps in the summer
And nobody puts down to die;
And Time then just goes on forever
And hearts then continue to beat
To the sound of the old moon-drum drumming
And the glide of Eternity's feet;

"Too much," he heard himself whisper. "Too much. I can't. Is this the way poems happen? And where does it come from? Is it done?" he wondered.

And not sure, he put his head back down and closed his eyes and there were these words:

Somewhere the old people wander
And linger themselves into noon
And sleep in the wheat fields yonder
To rise as fresh children with moon.
Somewhere the children, old, maunder
And know what it is to be dead
And turn in their weeping to ponder
Oblivious filed 'neath their bed.
And sit at the long dining table
Where Life makes a banquet of flesh,
Where dis-able makes itself able
And spoiled puts on new masks of fresh.

Somewhere a band is playing
Oh listen, oh listen, that tune!
If you learn it you'll dance on forever
In June . . .
And yet June . . .
And more . . . June . . .
And Death will be dumb and not clever
And Death will lie silent forever
In June and June and more June.

The darkness now was complete. The twilight was quiet.

He opened his eyes fully and lay staring at the ceiling in disbelief. He turned in the bed and picked up a picture postcard lying on the nightstand, and stared at the image.

At last he said, half aloud, "Am I happy?"

And responded to himself, "I am *not* happy."

Very slowly he got out of bed, dressed, went downstairs, walked to the train station, bought a ticket and took the first train heading west.

Chapter 3

Because.

Well, now, he thought, as he peered down the tracks. This place isn't on the map. But when the train slowed, I jumped, because . . .

He turned and saw a wind-battered sign over the flimsy station that seemed about to sink under tides of sand: SUMMERTON, ARIZONA.

"Yes, sir," said a voice.

The traveler dropped his gaze to find a man of some middle years with fair hair and clear eyes seated on the porch of the ramshackle station, leaning back in shadow. An assortment of hats hung above him, which read: TICKET SELLER, BAGGAGE MASTER, SWITCHMAN, NIGHT WATCHMAN, TAXI. Upon his head was a cap with the word STATIONMASTER stitched on its bill in bright red thread.

"What'll it be," the middle-aged man said, looking at the stranger steadily. "A ticket on the next train? Or a taxi two blocks over to the Egyptian View Arms?"

"God, I don't know." The younger man wiped his brow and blinked in all directions. "I just got here. Jumped off. Don't know why."

"Don't argue with impulse," said the stationmaster. "With luck you miss the frying pan and hit a nice cool lake on a hot day. So, what'll it be?"

The older man waited.

"Taxi, two blocks, to the Egyptian View Arms," said the young man, quickly. "Yes!"

"Fine, given the fact that there are no Egyptians to view, nor a Nile Delta. And Cairo, Illinois, is a thousand miles east. But I suppose we've got plenty of arms."

The old man rose, pulled the STATION MASTER cap from his head, and replaced it with the TAXI cap. He bent to take the small suitcase when the young man said, "You're not just going to leave—?"

"The station? It'll mind itself. The tracks aren't going nowhere, there's nothing to be purloined within, and it'll be some few days before another train takes us by surprise. Come on." He hoisted the bag and shuffled out of the gloom and around the corner.

Behind the station was no taxi. Instead, a rather handsome large white horse stood, patiently waiting.

And behind the horse was a small upright wagon with the words KELLY'S BAKERY, FRESH BREAD, painted on its side.

The taxi driver beckoned and the young man climbed into the wagon and settled himself in the warm shadow. The stranger inhaled.

"Ain't that a rare fine smell?" said the taxi driver. "Just delivered five dozen loaves!"

"That," said the young man, "is the perfume of Eden on the first morn."

The older man raised his eyebrows. "Well, now," he wondered, "what's a newspaper writer with aspirations to be a novelist doing in Summerton, Arizona?"

"Because," said the young man.

"Because?" said the older man. "That's one of the finest reasons in the world. Leaves lots of room for decisions." He climbed up onto the driver's seat, looked with gentle eyes at the waiting horse and made a soft clicking noise with his tongue and said, "Claude."

And the horse, hearing his name, carried them away into Summerton, Arizona.

Chapter 4

The air was hot as the bakery wagon moved and then, as they reached the shadows of trees, the air began to cool.

The young man leaned forward.

"How did you guess?"

"What?" said the driver.

"That I'm a writer," said the young man.

The taxi driver glanced at the passing trees and nodded.

"Your tongue improves your words on their way out. Keep talking."

"I've heard rumors about Summerton."

"Lots of folks *hear,* few arrive."

"I heard your town's another time and place, vanishing maybe. Surviving, I hope."

"Let me see your good eye," said the driver.

The reporter turned and looked straight on at him.

The driver nodded again.

"Nope, not yet jaundiced. I think you see what you look at, tell what you feel. Welcome. Name's Culpepper. Elias."

"Mr. Culpepper." The young man touched the older man's shoulder. "James Cardiff."

"Lord," said Culpepper. "Aren't we a pair? Culpepper and Cardiff. Could be genteel lawyers, architects, printers. Names like that don't come in tandems. Culpepper and, now, Cardiff."

And Claude the horse trotted a little more quickly through the shadows of trees.

The horse rambled through town, Elias Culpepper pointing right and left, chatting up a storm.

"There's the envelope factory. All our mail starts there. There's the steam works, once made steam, I forget what for. And right now, passing *Culpepper Summerton News.* If there's news once a month, we *print* it! Four pages in large, easy-to-read type. So you see, you and I are, in a way, in the same business. You don't, of course, also rein horses and punch rail tickets."

"I most certainly don't," said James Cardiff, and they both laughed quietly.

"And," said Elias Culpepper, as Claude rounded a curve into a lane where elms and oaks and maples fused the center and wove the sky in green and blue colors, a fine thatchwork above and below, "this is New Sunrise Way. Best families live here. That's the Ribtrees', there's the Townways'. And—"

"My God," said James Cardiff. "Those front *lawns. Look,* Mr. Culpepper!"

And they drove by fence after fence, where crowds of sunflowers lifted huge round clock faces to time the sun, to open with the dawn and close with the dusk, a hundred in this patch under an elm, two hundred in the next yard, and five hundred beyond.

Every curb was lined with the tall green stalks ending in vast dark faces and yellow fringes.

"It's like a crowd watching a parade," said James Cardiff.

"Come to think," said Elias Culpepper.

He gave a genteel wave of his hand.

"Now, Mr. Cardiff. You're the first reporter's visited in years. Nothing's happened here since 1903, the year of the *Small* Flood. Or 1902, if you want the *Big* One. Mr. Cardiff, what would a reporter be wanting with a town like this where nothing happens by the hour?"

"Something *might,*" said Cardiff, uneasily.

He raised his gaze and looked at the town all around. You're here, he thought, but maybe you won't be. I know, but won't tell. It's a terrible truth that may wipe you away. My mind is open, but my mouth is shut. The future is uncertain and unsure.

Mr. Culpepper pulled a stick of spearmint gum from his shirt pocket, peeled its wrapper, popped it in his mouth, and chewed.

"You *know* something *I* don't know, Mr. Cardiff?"

"Maybe," said Cardiff, "*you* know things about Summerton *you* haven't told *me*."

"Then I hope we both fess up soon."

And with that, Elias Culpepper reined Claude gently into the graveled driveway of the sunflower yard of a private home with a sign above the porch: EGYPTIAN VIEW ARMS. BOARDING.

And he had not lied.

No Nile River was in sight.

Chapter 5

At which moment an old-fashioned ice wagon with a full dark cavern mouth of frost entered the yard, led by a horse in dire need of his Antarctic cargo. Cardiff could taste the ice, from thirty summers long gone.

"Just in time," said the iceman. "Hot day. Go grab." He nodded toward the rear of his wagon.

Cardiff, on pure instinct, jumped down from the bread wagon and went straight to the back of the ice wagon, and felt his ten-year-old hand reach in and grab a sharp icicle. He stepped back and rubbed it on his brow. His other hand instinctively took a handkerchief from his pocket to wrap the ice. Sucking it, he moved away.

"How's it taste?" he heard Culpepper say.

Cardiff gave the ice another lick.

"Linen."

Only then did he glance back at the street.

It was such a street as could not be believed. There was not a roof on any house that had not been freshly tarred and lathed or tiled. Not a porch swing that did not hang straight. Not a window that did not shine like a mirrored shield in Valhalla halls, all gold at sunrise and sunset, all clear running brookstream at noon. Not a bay window that did not display books leaning against others' quiet wits on inner library shelves. Not a rain funnel spout without its rain barrel gathering the seasons. Not a backyard that was not, this day, filled with carpets being flailed so that time dusted on the wind and old patterns sprung forth to rococo new. Not a kitchen that did not send forth promises of hunger placated and easy evenings of contemplation on victuals contained just south-southwest of the soul.

All, all perfect, all painted, all fresh, all new, all beautiful, a perfect town in a perfect blend of silence and unseen hustle and flurry.

"A penny for your thoughts," said Elias Culpepper.

Cardiff shook his head, his eyes shut, because he had seen nothing, but imagined much.

"I can't tell you," said Cardiff, in a whisper.

"Try," said Elias Culpepper.

Cardiff shook his head again, nearly suffering with inexplicable happiness.

Peeling the handkerchief from around the ice, he put the last sliver in his mouth and gave it a crunch as he started up the porch steps with his back to the town, wondering what he would find next.

Chapter 6

James Cardiff stood in quiet amazement.

The front porch of the Egyptian View Arms was the longest he had ever seen. It had so many white wicker rockers he stopped counting. Occupying some of the rockers was an assortment of youngish not quite middle-aged gentlemen, nattily dressed, with slicked-back hair, fresh out of the shower. And interspersed among the men were late-thirties-not-yet-forty women in summer dresses looking as if they had all been cut from the same rose or orchid or gardenia wallpaper. The men had haircuts each sheared by the same barber. The women wore their tresses like bright helmets designed by some Parisian, ironed and curlicued long before Cardiff had been born. And the assembly of rockers all tilted forward and then back, in unison, in a quiet surf, as if the same ocean breeze moved them all, soundless and serene.

As Cardiff put his foot on the porch landing, all the rocking stopped, all the faces lifted, and there was a blaze of smiles and every hand rose in a quiet wave of welcome. He nodded and the white summer wickers refloated themselves, and a murmur of conversation began.

Looking at the long line of handsome people, he thought: *Strange, so many men home at this hour of the day. Most peculiar.*

A tiny crystal bell tinkled in the dim screen doorway.

"Soup's on," a woman's voice called.

In a matter of seconds, the wicker chairs emptied, as all the summer people filed through the screen door with a hum.

He was about to follow when he stopped, turned his head and looked back.

"What?" he whispered.

Elias Culpepper was at his elbow, gently placing Cardiff's suitcase beside him.

"That sound," said Cardiff. "Somewhere . . ."

Elias Culpepper laughed quietly. "That's the town band rehearsing Thursday night's performance of the short-form *Tosca.* When she jumps it only takes two minutes for her to land."

"*Tosca,*" said Cardiff, and listened to the far brass music. "Somewhere . . ."

"Step in," said Culpepper, who held the screen door wide for James Cardiff.

Chapter 7

Inside the dim hall, Cardiff felt as if he had moved into a summer-cool milk shed that smelled of large canisters of cream hidden away from the sun, and iceboxes dripping their secret liquors, and bread laid out fresh on kitchen tables, and pies cooling on windowsills.

Cardiff took another step and knew he would sleep nine hours a night here and wake like a boy at dawn, excited that he was alive, and all the world beginning, morn after morn, glad for his heart in his body, and his pulse in his wrists.

He heard someone laughing. And it was himself, overwhelmed with a joy he could not explain.

There was the merest motion from somewhere high in the house. Cardiff looked up.

Descending the stairs, and pausing now at seeing him, was the most beautiful woman in the world.

Somewhere, sometime, he had heard someone say: Fix the image before it fades. So said the first cameras that trapped light and carried that illumination to obscuras where chemicals laid out in porcelain caused the trapped ghosts to rouse. Faces caught at noon were summoned up out of sour baths to reestablish their eyes, their mouths, and then the haunting flesh of beauty or arrogance, or the impatience of a child held still. In darkness the phantoms lurked in chemicals until some gestures surfaced them out of time into a forever that could be held in the hands long after the warm flesh had vanished.

It was thus and so with this woman, this bright noon wonder who descended the stairs into the cool shadow of the hall only to reemerge in a shaft of sunlight in the dining room door. Her hand drifted to take Cardiff's hand, and then her wrist and arm and shoulder and at last, as from that chemistry in an obscura room, the ghost of a face so lovely it burst on him like a flower when the dawn causes it to widen its beauty. Her measuring bright and summer-electric eyes shone merrily, watching him, as if he, too, had just arisen from those miraculous tides in which memory swims, as if to say: Remember me?

I do! he thought.

Yes? he thought he heard her say.

Yes! he cried, not speaking. *I always hoped I might remember you.*

Well, then, her eyes said, *we shall be friends. Perhaps in another time, we met.*

"They're waiting for us," she said aloud.

Yes, he thought, *for* both *of us!*

And now he spoke. "Your name?"

But you already know it, her silence replied.

And it was the name of a woman dead these four thousand years and lost in Egyptian sands, and now refreshed at noon in another desert near an empty station and silent tracks.

"Nefertiti," he said. "A fine name. It means the Beautiful One Is Here."

"Ah," she said, "you know."

"Tutankhamen came from the tomb when I was three," he said. "I saw his golden mask and wanted my face to be his."

"But it is," she said. "You just never noticed."

"Can I believe that?"

"Believe it and it will happen in the midst of your belief. Are you hungry?"

Starved, he thought, staring at her.

"Before you fall," she laughed, "come."

And she led him in to a feasting of summer gods.

Chapter 8

The dining room, like the porch, was the longest one he'd ever seen.

All of the summer porch people were lined up on either side of an incredible table, staring at Cardiff and Nef as they came through the door.

At the far end were two chairs waiting for them and as soon as Cardiff and Nef sat, there was a flurry of activity as utensils were raised and platters passed.

There was an incredible salad, an amazing omelet, and a soup smooth as velvet. From the kitchen drifted a scent that promised a dessert sweet as ambrosia.

In the middle of his astonishment, Cardiff said, "Hold on, this is too much. I must see."

He rose and walked to a door at the end of the dining room, which opened into the kitchen.

Entering the kitchen, he stared across the room at what seemed a familiar doorway.

He knew where it led.

The pantry.

And not just any pantry, but his grandmother's pantry, or something just like it. How could that be?

He stepped forward and pushed the door, half-expecting that he would find his grandmother within, lost in that special jungle where hung leopard bananas, where doughnuts were buried in quicksands of powdered sugar. Where apples shone in bins and peaches displayed their warm summer cheeks. Where row on row, shelf on shelf, of condiments and spices rose to an always-twilight ceiling.

He heard himself intoning the names that he read off the jar labels, the monikers of Indian princes and Arabian wanderers.

Cardimon and anise and cinnamon were there, and cayenne and curry. Added to which there were ginger and paprika and thyme and celandrine.

He could almost have sung the syllables and awakened at night to hear himself humming the sounds all over again.

He scanned and re-scanned the shelves, took a deep breath, and turned, looking back into the kitchen, sure he would find a familiar shape bent over the table, preparing the last courses for the amazing lunch.

He saw a portly woman icing a buttery yellow cake with dark chocolate, and he thought if he cried her name, his grandmother might turn and rush to hold him.

But he said nothing and watched the woman finish the job with a flourish, and hand the cake to a maid who carried it out into the dining room.

He went back to join Nef, his appetite gone, having fed himself in the pantry wilderness, which was more than enough.

Nef, he thought, gazing at her, is a woman of all women, a beauty of all beauties. That wheat field painted again and again by Monet that became *the* wheat field. That church façade similarly painted, again and again, until it was the most perfect façade in the history of churches. That bright apple and fabled orange by Cézanne that never fades.

"Mr. Cardiff," he heard her say. "Sit, eat. You mustn't keep me waiting. I've been waiting too many years."

He drew close, not able to take his eyes away from her.

"Great god," he said. "How old are you?"

"*You* tell me," she said.

"Oh, hell," he cried. "You were born maybe twenty years ago. Thirty. Or the day before yesterday."

"I am all of those."

"How?"

"I am your sister, your daughter, and someone you knew years ago back in school, yes? I am the girl you asked to the Senior Prom but she had promised another."

"That's my life. That happened. How did you guess?"

"I never guess," she replied. "I *know.* The important thing is that you're here at last."

"You sound as if you expected me."

"Forever," she said.

"But I didn't know I was coming here until last night, in the middle of a dream. I fixed my mind only at the last moment. I decided to write a story . . ."

She laughed quietly. "How can that be? It sounds so like those unhealthy romances written by healthy housewives. What made you choose Summerton? Was it our name?"

"I saw a postcard someone must have picked up on their way through."

"Oh, that would have been years ago."

"It looked like a nice town—a friendly spot for tourists looking for a place to relax, enjoy the desert air. But then, I looked for it on the map. And you know what? It's not on any map I could find."

"Well, the train doesn't stop here."

"It didn't stop today," he admitted. "Only two things got off: me and my suitcase."

"You travel lightly."

"I'm just here overnight. When the next train runs through, not stopping, I'll grab on."

"No," she said softly. "That's not how it's supposed to be."

"I've got to go home and finish my story," he insisted.

"Ah, yes," she said. "And what will you say about this town that no one can find?"

A cloud crossed the sky and the dining room windows darkened, and a shadow fell across his face. There were two truths to tell, but he could tell only one.

"That it's a lovely town," he said, lamely. "The kind that doesn't exist anymore. That people should remember and celebrate. But how did you know I was coming?"

"I woke at dawn," she said. "I heard your train from a long way off. By noon the train was just beyond the mountains, and I heard its whistle."

"And did you expect someone named Cardiff?"

"Cardiff?" she wondered. "There was a giant, once—"

"In all the newspapers. A fraud."

"And," she said. "Are *you* a fraud?"

He could not meet her gaze.

Chapter 9

When he looked up, Nef's chair was empty. The other diners, too, had all left the table, gone back to their rocking chairs or, perhaps, to summer afternoon naps.

"Lord," he murmured. "That woman, young, but how young? Old, but how old?"

Suddenly Elias Culpepper touched his elbow.

"You want a real tour of our town? Claude needs to deliver some more fresh-baked bread. On your feet!"

The wagon was loaded with a redolent harvest. The warm loaves had been neatly stacked row on row within the oven-smelling wagon, thirty or forty loaves in all, with names lettered on the wax-paper wrappings. Beside these were waxed boxes of muffins and cakes, carefully tied with string.

Cardiff took three immense inhalations and almost fell with the overconsumption.

Culpepper handed him a small packet and a knife.

"What's this?" said Cardiff.

"You won't be a block away before the bread overcomes you. This is a butter knife. This here is a full loaf. Don't bring it back."

"It'll ruin my supper."

"No. Enhance. Summer outside. Summer inside."

He handed over a pad with names and addresses.

"Just in case," said Culpepper.

"You're sending me out on my own? How do I know where to go?"

"Don't you worry. Claude knows the way. Never got lost yet. Right, Claude?"

Claude looked back, neither amused nor serious, just *ready.*

"Just go easy on the reins. Claude's got his own system. You just tag along. It's the only way to see the town without any jabber from me. Giddap."

Cardiff jumped aboard. Claude tugged, the wagon lurched forward.

"Hell." He fumbled with the notebook, scanning the names and addresses. "What's the first stop?"

"Git!"

The bread wagon drifted away, warming the air with the heady scents of yeast and grain.

Claude trotted as if he could hardly wait to be right.

Chapter 10

Claude jogged at a goodly pace for two blocks and turned sweetly to the right.

His eyes twitched toward a front yard mailbox: *Abercrombie.*

Cardiff checked his list.

Abercrombie!

"Damn!"

He jumped from the wagon, loaf in hand, when a woman's voice called, "Thank you, Claude."

A woman of some forty years stood at the gate to take the bread. "You, too, of course," she said. "Mister . . .?"

"Cardiff, ma'm."

"Claude," she called, "take good care of Mr. Cardiff. And Mr. Cardiff, you take good care of Claude. Morning!"

And the wagon jounced along the bricks under a congress of trees that laced themselves to lattice out the sun.

"Fillmore's next." Cardiff eyed the list, ready to pull on the reins when the horse stopped at a second gate.

Cardiff popped the bread in the Fillmore mailbox and raced to catch up with Claude, who had resumed his route without waiting for his driver.

So it went. Bramble. Jones. Williams. Isaacson. Meredith. Bread. Cake. Bread. Muffins. Bread. Cake. Bread.

Claude turned a final corner.

And there was a school.

"Hold up, Claude!"

Cardiff alighted and walked into the schoolyard to find a teeter-totter, its old blue paint flaking, next to an old swingset, its splintery wooden seats suspended from rusted iron chains.

"Well, now," whispered Cardiff.

The school was two stories high. Its double doors were shut, and all eight of its windows were crusted with dust.

Cardiff rattled the front doors. Locked tight.

"It's only May," Cardiff said to himself. "School's not out yet."

Claude whinnied irritably, and perhaps out of pique, began a slow glide away from the school.

"Claude!" Cardiff put iron in it. "Stay!"

Claude stayed, drumming the bricks with both forefeet.

Cardiff turned back to the building. Carved in the lintel, above the main door were the words: SUMMERTON GRAMMAR SCHOOL, DEDICATED JANUARY IST, 1888.

"Eighteen eighty-eight," Cardiff muttered. "Well, now."

He gave one last look at the dust-caked windows and the rusted swing chains and said, "One last go-round, Claude."

Claude did not move.

"We're all out of bread and names, is that it? You only take bakery orders, nothing else?"

Even Claude's shadow did not move.

"Well, we'll just stand here until you do me a favor. Your new star boarder wants to cross-section the whole blasted town. What's it to be? No water, no oats, without a full trot."

Water and oats did it.

Full trot.

They sailed down Clover Avenue and up Hibiscus Way and over on to Rosewood Place and right on Juneglade and left again on Sandalwood then Ravine, which ran off the edge of a shallow ravine cut by ancient rains. He stared at lawn after lawn after lawn, all of them lush, green, perfect. No baseball bats. No baseballs. No basketball hoops. No basketballs. No tennis rackets. No croquet mallets. No hopscotch chalk marks on sidewalks. No tire swings on trees.

Claude trotted him back to the Egyptian View Arms, where Elias Culpepper was waiting.

Cardiff climbed down from the bread wagon.

"Well?"

Cardiff looked back at the summer drift of green lawns and green hedges and golden sunflowers and said, "Where are the children?"

Chapter 11

Mr. Culpepper did not immediately respond.

For dead ahead there was afternoon high tea, with apricot and peach tarts and strawberry delight and coffee instead of tea and then port instead of coffee and then there was dinner, a real humdinger, that lasted until well after nine and then the inhabitants of the Egyptian View Arms headed up, one by one, to their most welcome cool summer night beds, and Cardiff sat out on the croquetless and hoopless lawn, watching Mr. Culpepper on the porch, smoking several small bonfire pipes, waiting.

At last Cardiff, in full brooding pace, arrived at the bottom of the porch rail and waited.

"You were asking about no children?" said Elias Culpepper.

Cardiff nodded.

"A good reporter wouldn't allow so much time to pass after asking such an important question."

"More time is passing right now," said Cardiff, gently, climbing the porch steps.

"So it is. Here."

A bottle of wine and two small snifters sat on the railing.

Cardiff drained his at a jolt, and went to sit next to Elias Culpepper.

Culpepper puffed smoke. "We have," he said, seeming to consider his words with care, "sent all the children away to school."

Cardiff stared. "The whole town? Every child?"

"That's the sum. It's a hundred miles to Phoenix in one direction. Two hundred to Tucson. Nothing but sand and petrified forest in between. The children need schools with proper trees. We got proper trees here, yes, but we can't hire teachers to teach here. We did, at one time, but they got too lonesome. They wouldn't come, so our children had to go."

"If I came back in late June would I meet the kids coming home for the summer?"

Culpepper held still, much like Claude.

"I said—"

"I heard." Culpepper knocked the sparking ash from his pipe. "If I said yes, would you believe me?"

Cardiff shook his head.

"You implying I'm a mile off from the truth?"

"I'm only implying," Cardiff said, "that we are at a taffy pull. I'm waiting to see how far you pull it."

Culpepper smiled.

"The children aren't coming home. They have chosen summer school in Amherst, Providence, and Sag Harbor. One is even in Mystic Seaport. Ain't that a fine sound? Mystic. I sat there once in a thunderstorm reading every other chapter of *Moby-Dick*."

"The children are not coming home," said Cardiff. "Can I guess why?"

The older man nodded, pipe in mouth, unlit.

Cardiff took out his notepad and stared at it.

"The children of this town," he said at last, "won't come home. Not one. None. Never."

He closed the notepad and continued: "The reason why the children are never coming home is," he swallowed hard, "there *are* no children. Something happened a long time ago, God knows what, but it happened. And this town is a town of no family homecomings. The last child left long ago, or the last child finally grew up. And you're one of them."

"Is that a question?"

"No," said Cardiff. "An answer."

Culpepper leaned back in his chair and shut his eyes. "You," he said, the smoke long gone from his pipe, "are an A-1 Four Star Headline News Reporter."

Chapter 12

"I . . .," said Cardiff.

"Enough," Culpepper interrupted. "For tonight."

He held out another glass of bright amber wine. Cardiff drank. When he looked up, the front screen door of the Egyptian View Arms tapped shut. Someone went upstairs. His ambiance stayed.

Cardiff refilled his glass.

"Never coming home. Never ever," he whispered.

And went up to bed.

Sleep well, someone said somewhere in the house. But he could not sleep. He lay, fully dressed, doing philosophical sums on the ceiling, erasing, adding, erasing again until he sat up abruptly and looked out across the meadow town of thousands of flowers in the midst of which houses rose and sank only to rise again, ships on a summer sea.

I will arise and go now, thought Cardiff, but not to a bee-loud glade. Rather, to a place of earthen silence and the sounds of death's-head moths on powdery wings.

He slipped down the front hall stairs barefoot and once outside, let the screen door tap shut silently and, sitting on the lawn, put on his shoes as the moon rose.

Good, he thought, I won't need a flashlight.

In the middle of the street he looked back. Was there someone at the screen door, a shadow, watching? He walked and then began to jog.

Imagine that you are Claude, he thought, his breath coming in quick pants. Turn here, now there, now another right and—

The graveyard.

All that cold marble crushed his heart and stopped his breathing. There was no iron fence around the burial park.

He entered silently and bent to touch the first gravestone. His fingers brushed the name: BIANCA SHERMAN BATES

And the date: BORN, JULY 3, 1882

And below that: *R.I.P.*

But no date of death.

The clouds covered the moon. He moved on to the next stone.

WILLIAM HENRY CLAY

1885 –

R.I.P.

And again, no mortal date.

He brushed a third gravestone and found:

HENRIETTA PARKS

August 13, 1881

Gone to God

But, Cardiff knew, she had not as yet gone to God.

The moon darkened and then took strength from itself. It shone upon a small Grecian tomb not fifty feet away, a lodge of exquisite architecture, a miniature Acropolis upheld by four vestal virgins, or goddesses, beautiful maidens, wondrous women. His heart pulsed. All four marble women seemed suddenly alive, as if the pale light had awakened them, and they might step forth, unclad, into the tableau of named and dateless stones.

He sucked in his breath. His heart pulsed again.

For as he watched, one of the goddesses, one of the forever-beautiful maidens, trembled with the night chill and shifted out into the moonlight.

He could not tell if he was terrified or delighted. After all, it was late at night in this yard of the dead.

But she? She was naked to the weather, or almost; a mist of silk covered her breasts and plumed around her waist as she drifted away from the other pale statues.

She moved among the stones, silent as the marble she had been but now was not, until she stood before him with her dark hair tousled about her small ears and her great eyes the color of lilacs. She raised her hand tenderly and smiled.

"You," he whispered. "What are *you* doing here?"

She replied quietly, "Where else *should* I be?"

She held out her hand and led him in silence out of the graveyard.

Looking back he saw the abandoned puzzle of names and enigma of dates.

Everyone born, he thought, *but none has died. The stones are blank, waiting for someone to date their ghosts bound for Eternity.*

"Yes?" someone said. But her lips had not moved.

And you followed me, he thought, *to stop me from reading the gravestones and asking questions. And what about the absent children, never coming home?*

And as if they glided on ice, on a vast sea of moonlight, they arrived where a crowd of sunflowers hardly stirred as they passed and their feet were soundless, moving up the path to the porch and across the porch, and up the stairs, one, two, three floors until they reached a tower room where the door stood wide to reveal a bed as bright as a glacier, its covers thrown back, all snow on a hot summer night.

Yes, she said.

He sleepwalked the rest of the way. Behind him, he saw his clothes, like the discards of a careless child, strewn on the parquetry. He stood by the snowbank bed and thought, *One last question. The graveyard. Are there bodies beneath the stones? Is anyone there?*

But it was too late. Even as he opened his mouth to question, he tumbled into the snow.

And he was drowning in whiteness, crying out as he inhaled the light and then out of the rushing storm, a warmness came; he was touched and held, but could not see what or who held him, and he relaxed, drowned.

When next he woke, he was not swimming but floating. Somehow he had leaped from a cliff, and someone with him, unseen, as he soared up until lightning struck, tore at him in half terror, half joy, to fall and strike the bed with his entire body and his soul.

When he awoke again, the storm over, and the flying gone, he found a small hand in his, and without opening his eyes he knew that *she* lay beside him, her breath keeping time with his. It was not yet dawn.

She spoke.

"Was there something you wanted to ask?"

"Tomorrow," he whispered. "I'll ask you then."

"Yes," she said quietly. "Then."

Then, for the first time, it seemed, her mouth touched his.

Chapter 13

He awoke to the sun pouring in through the high attic window. Questions gathered behind his tongue.

Beside him, the bed was empty.

Gone.

Afraid of the truth? he wondered.

No, he thought, *she will have left a note on the icebox door.* Somehow he knew. *Go look.*

The note was there.

Mr. Cardiff:

Many tourists arriving. I must welcome them. Questions at breakfast.

Nef.

Far off, wasn't there the merest wail of a locomotive whistle, the softest churn of some great engine?

On the front porch, Cardiff listened, and again the faint locomotive cry stirred beyond the horizon.

He glanced up at the top floor. Had she fled toward that sound? Had the boarders heard, too?

He ran down to the rail station and stood in the middle of the blazing hot iron tracks, daring the whistle to sound again. But this time, silence.

Separate trains bringing what? he wondered.

I arrived first, he thought, the one who tries to be good.

And what comes next?

He waited, but the air remained silent and the horizon line serene, so he walked back to the Egyptian View Arms.

There were boarders in every window, waiting. "It's all right," he called. "It was nothing."

Someone called down from above, quietly, "Are you *sure*?"

Chapter 14

Nef was not at breakfast, or lunch, or dinner. He went to bed hungry.

Chapter 15

At midnight the wind blew softly in the window, whispering the curtains, shadowing the moonlight.

There, far across town, lay the cemetery, immense white teeth scattered on a meadow of fresh moon-silvered grass.

Four dozen stones dead, but not dead.

All lies, he thought.

And found himself halfway down the boarding house stairs, surrounded by the exhalations of sleeping people. There was no sound save the drip of the ice pan under the icebox in the moonlit kitchen. The house brimmed with lemon and lilac illumination from the candied windows over the front entrance.

He found himself on the dusty road, alone with his shadow.

He found himself at the cemetery gate.

In the middle of the graveyard, he found a shovel in his hands.

He dug until . . .

There was a hollow thud under the dust.

He worked swiftly, clearing away the earth, and bent to tug at the edge of the coffin, at which moment he heard a single sound.

A footstep.

Yes! he thought wildly, happily.

She's here again. She had to come find me, and take me home. She . . .

His heartbeat hammered and then slowed.

Slowly, Cardiff rose by the open grave.

Elias Culpepper stood by the iron gate, trying to figure out just what to say to Cardiff, who was digging where no one should dig.

Cardiff let the spade fall. "Mr. Culpepper?"

Elias Culpepper responded. "Oh God, God, go on. Lift the lid. *Do* it!" And when Cardiff hesitated, said, "Now!"

Cardiff bent and pulled at the coffin lid. It was neither nailed nor locked. He swung back the lid and stared down into the coffin.

Elias Culpepper came to stand beside him.

They both stared down at . . .

An empty coffin.

"I suspect," said Elias Culpepper, "you are in need of a drink."

"Two," said Cardiff, "would be fine."

Chapter 16

They were smoking fine cigars and drinking nameless wine in the middle of the night. Cardiff leaned back in his wicker chair, eyes tight shut.

"You been noticing things?" inquired Elias Culpepper.

"A baker's dozen. When Claude took me on the bread and muffin tour I couldn't help but notice there are no signs—anywhere—for doctors. Not one funeral parlor that I could see."

"Must be somewhere," said Culpepper.

"How come not in the phone book yellow pages? No doctors, no surgeons, no mortuary offices."

"An oversight."

Cardiff studied his notes.

"Lord, you don't even have a hospital in this almost ghost town!"

"We got one small one."

Cardiff underlined an entry on his list. "An out-patient clinic thirty feet square? Is that *all* that ever happens, so you don't *need* a *big* facility?"

"That," said Culpepper, "would about describe it."

"All you ever have is cut fingers, bee-stings, and the occasional sprained ankle?"

"You've whittled it down fine," said the other, "but that's the sum. Continue."

"That," said Cardiff, gazing down on the town from the high verandah, "that tells why all the gravestones are unfinished and all the coffins empty!"

"You only dug *one* up."

"I don't need to open more. *Do* I?"

Quietly, Culpepper shook his head.

"Hell, Mr. Culpepper," said Cardiff. "I'm speechless!"

"To tell the truth," said Culpepper, "so am I. This is the first time anyone has ever asked what you've been asking. We folks have been so busy just living, we never figured anyone would come, gather his spit, grab a spade, and dig!"

"I apologize."

"Now you'll want a practical history. I'll give it to you. Write it down, Mr. Cardiff, write it down. Over the years, when visitors arrived, they got bored quick, and left even quicker. We tried to *look* like every other town. We put on nice false-front funerals, hearse and all, real flowers, live organ music, but empty coffins with shut lids, just to impress. We were going to hold a pretend funeral tomorrow, show off, so you'd be assured we sometimes die—"

"Sometimes?!" cried Cardiff.

"Well, it has been a while. Cars occasionally run over us. Someone might fall from a ladder."

"No diseases, whooping cough, pneumonia?"

"We don't whoop and we don't cough. We wear out . . . slow."

"How slow?"

"Oh, at last count, just about—"

"How slow?!"

"One hundred, two hundred years."

"Which?"

"We figure about two hundred. It's still too early to tell. We've only been at this since 1864, '65, Lincoln's time."

"All of you?"

"All."

"Nef, too?"

"Wouldn't lie."

"But she's younger than I am!"

"Your grandma, maybe."

"My God!"

"God put us up to it. But it's the weather, mostly. And, well now, the wine."

Cardiff stared at his empty glass.

"The wine makes you live to two hundred?!"

"Unless it kills you before breakfast. Finish your glass, Mr. Cardiff, finish your glass."

Chapter 17

Elias Culpepper leaned forward to scan Cardiff's notepad.

"You got any more doubts, indecisions, or opinions?"

Cardiff mused over his notes. "There don't seem to be any roaring businesses in Summerton."

"A few mice but no buffalo."

"No travel agencies, just a train station about to sink in the dust. Main road is mostly potholes. No one seems to leave, and very few arrive. How in Hades do you all survive?"

"Think." Culpepper sucked on his pipe.

"I am, dammit!"

"You heard about the lilies of the field. We toil not, neither do we spin. Just like you. You don't have to move, do you? On occasion, maybe, like tonight. But mostly you travel back and forth between your ears. Yes?"

"My God!" Cardiff cried, clutching his notepad. "Hideaways. Loners. Recluses. By the scores of dozens. You're writers!"

"You can say that again."

"Writers!"

"In every room, attic, broom-closet, or basement, both sides of the street right out to the edge of town."

"The whole town, everybody?"

"All but a few lazy illiterates."

"That's unheard of."

"You heard it now."

"Salzburg, a town full of musicians, composers, conductors. Geneva, chock-full of bankers, clockmakers, walking wounded ski dropouts. Nantucket, once anyway, ships, sailors, and whale-widow wives. But this, *this*!"

Cardiff jumped up and stared wildly toward the midnight town.

"Don't listen for typewriters," advised Culpepper. "Just quiet things."

Pens, pencils, pads, paper, thought Cardiff. *Whispers of lead or ink. Summer quiet thoughts on summer quiet noons.*

"Writers," murmured Cardiff, spying this house or that, across the street, "never have to get up and go. And no one knows what color you are, by mail, or what sex, or how tall or how short. Could be a company of midgets, a sideshow of giants. Writers. Godfrey Daniel!"

"Watch your language."

Cardiff turned to stare down at his companion. "But they can't all be successful?"

"Mostly."

"Would I know any of their names?"

"If I told you, but I won't."

"A beehive of talent." Cardiff exhaled. "But how did they all wind up here?"

"Genes, chromosomes, need. You've heard of those little writers' colonies? Well, this one's big. We're soul mates. Similar people. Nobody laughing at what someone else writes. No alcoholics, however, no bats out of hell, or wild parties."

"F. Scott Fitzgerald can't get in?"

"Better not try."

"Sounds boring."

"Only if you lose your pad and pencil."

"You one of them?"

"In my own quiet way."

"A poet!"

"Not so loud. Someone might hear."

"A poet," Cardiff whispered.

"Mostly haiku. At midnight when I put on my specs and reach for my pen. Semi-haiku, too many beats."

"Example?"

Culpepper recited:

Oh, cat that I truly love,
Oh, hummingbird that I madly love.
What are you doing in the cat's mouth?

Cardiff whooped with delight. "I never could write that!"

"Don't try. Just *do.*"

"I'll be damned. More!"

A pillow of snow by my warm face.
A snowdrift at my touch;
You are gone.

Culpepper quietly reloaded his pipe to cover his embarrassment.

"I don't recite that one often. Sad."

To break the quiet, Cardiff said: "How do you writers stay in touch with the outside world?"

Culpepper stared off into the distance toward the empty train tracks beyond the silent road.

"I take a truck full of manuscripts to Gila Springs once a month, so we mail out from where we are *not,* bring back windfalls of checks, snowfalls of rejections. The wheat and chaff go into our bank, with its one teller and one president. The money waits there, in case some day we have to move."

Cardiff felt sweat suddenly break out all over his body.

"You got something to say, Mr. Cardiff?"

"Soon."

"I won't push." Culpepper relit his pipe and recited:

A mother remembers her dead son.
Today how far might he have wandered,
My mighty hunter of dragonflies.

"That's not mine. Wish it were. Japanese. Been around forever."

Cardiff paced back and forth on the porch and then turned.

"Good grief, it all fits. Writing is the only activity that could support a town like this, so far off. Like a mail order business."

"Writing *is* a mail order business. Anything you want you write a check, send it off, and before you know it, the Johnson Smith Company in Racine, Wisconsin, sends you what you need. Seebackoscopes. Gyroscopes. Mardi Gras masks. Orphan Annie dolls. Film clips from *The Hunch- back of Notre Dame.* Vanishing cards. Reappearing skeletons."

"All that *good* stuff." Cardiff smiled.

"All that good stuff."

They laughed quietly together.

Cardiff exhaled. "So, this is a writers' township."

"Thinking about staying?"

"No, about *leaving.*"

Cardiff stopped and put his hand over his mouth as if he had said something he shouldn't have said.

"Now what does that mean?" Elias Culpepper almost started up from his chair.

But before Cardiff could speak, a pale figure appeared on the lawn below the porch and started to climb the steps.

Cardiff called her name.

By the door the daughter of Elias Culpepper spoke. "When you're ready, come upstairs."

When I'm ready!? Cardiff thought wildly. *When I'm* ready!

The screen door shut.

"You'll need this," said Elias Culpepper.

He held out a last drink, which Cardiff took.

Chapter 18

Again, the large bed was a bank of snow on a warm summer night. She lay on one side, looking up at the ceiling, and did not move. He sat on the far edge, saying nothing, and at last tilted over and lay his head on the pillow, and waited.

Finally Nef said, "It seems to me you've spent a lot of time in the town graveyard since you arrived. Looking for what?"

He scanned the empty ceiling and replied.

"It seems to me you've been down at that train station where hardly any trains arrive. Why?"

She did not turn, but said, "It seems both of us are looking for something but won't or can't say why or what."

"So it seems."

Another silence. Now, at last, she looked at him.

"Which of us is going to confess?"

"You go first."

She laughed quietly.

"My truth is bigger and more incredible than yours."

He joined her laughter but shook his head. "Oh, no, my truth is more terrible."

She quickened and he felt her trembling.

"Don't frighten me."

"I don't want to. But there it is. And if tell you, I'm afraid you'll run and I won't ever see you again."

"Ever?" murmured Nef.

"Ever."

"Then," she said, "tell me what you can, but don't make me afraid."

But at that moment, far away in the night world, there was a single cry of a train, a locomotive, drawing near.

"Did you hear that? Is that the train that comes to take you away?"

There was a second cry of a whistle over the horizon.

"No," he said, "maybe it's the train that comes, God I hope not, with terrible news."

Slowly she sat up on the edge of the bed, her eyes shut. "I have to know."

"No," he said. "Don't go. Let me."

"But first . . .," she murmured.

Her hand gently pulled him over to her side of the bed.

Chapter 19

Sometime during the night, he sensed that he was once more alone.

He woke in a panic, at dawn, thinking, *I've missed the train. It's come and gone. But, no—*

He heard the locomotive whistle shrieking across the sky, moaning like a funeral train as the sun rose over desert sands.

Did he or did he not hear a bag, similar to his own, catapult from a not-stopping train to bang the station platform?

Did he or did he not hear someone landing like a three-hundred-pound anvil on the platform boards?

And then Cardiff knew. He let his head fall as if chopped. "Dear God, oh dear vengeful God!"

Chapter 20

They stood on the platform of the empty station, Cardiff at one end, the tall man at the other.

"James Edward McCoy?" Cardiff said.

"Cardiff," said McCoy, "is that you?"

Both smiled false smiles.

"What are you doing here?" said Cardiff.

"You might have known I would follow," said James Edward McCoy. "When you left town, I knew someone had died, and you'd gone to give him a proper burial. So I packed my bag."

"Why would you do that?"

"To keep you honest. I learned long ago you leaned one way, me the other. You were always wrong, I was always right. I hate liars."

"'Optimists' is the word you want."

"No *wonder* I hate you. The world's a cesspool and you keep swimming in it, heading for shore. Dear God, where *is* the shore? You'll never find it because the shore doesn't exist! We're rats drowning in a sewer, but you see lighthouses where there are none. You claim the *Titanic* is Mark Twain's steamboat. To you Svengali, Raskolnikov, and Hitler were the Three Stooges! I feel sorry for you. So I'm here to make you honest."

"Since when have you believed in honesty?"

"Honesty, currency, and common sense. Never play funhouse slot machines, don't toss red-hot pennies to the poor, or throw your landlady downstairs. Fine futures? Hell, the future's *now*, and it's rotten. So, just what are you up to in this jerkwater town?"

McCoy glared around the deserted station.

Cardiff said, "You'd better leave on the next train."

"I got twenty-four hours to steal your story." McCoy squinted at the shut sunflowers that lined the road into town. "Lead the way. I'll follow and trip over the bodies."

McCoy hoisted his bag and began to walk, and Cardiff, after a beat or two, jogged to catch up with him.

"My editor said I'd better come back with a headline—one thousand bucks if it's good, three if it's super." As they walked, McCoy surveyed the porch swings motionless in the early morning breeze and the high windows that reflected no light. "You know, this feels like super."

Cardiff trudged along, thinking: *Don't breathe. Lie low.*

The town heard.

No leaf trembled. No fruit fell. Shadows of dogs lay under bushes, but no dogs. The grass flattened like the fur on a nervous cat. All was stillness.

Pleased with the silence he sensed he had caused, McCoy stopped where two streets intersected, panoplied by trees. He stared at the green architecture and mused, "I get it." He dropped his bag, pulled a pencil from his shirt pocket, which he licked, and began to scribble in a notepad, pronouncing the syllables as he wrote. "Leftover town. Stillborn, Nebraska. Remembrance, Ohio. Steamed west in 1880, lost steam 1890. End of the line 1900. Long lost."

Cardiff suffered lockjaw.

McCoy appraised him. "I'm on the money, right? I can see it in your face. You came to bury Caesar. I came to stir his bones. You followed your intuition here; I came thanks to an itching hunch. You liked what you saw and probably would have gone home and said nothing. I *don't* like what I see, past tense." He stuck the pencil behind his ear, jammed the notepad in his pants pocket, and reached down to heft his bag once more. As if propelled by the sound of his own voice, he continued striding down Summerton's streets, proclaiming as he went, "Look at that lousy architecture, the gimcrack scrimshaw rococo baroque shingles and hang-ons. You ever see so many damn scroll-cut wooden icicles? Christ, wouldn't it be awful to be trapped here forever, even just *two* weeks every summer? Hey, now, what's *this*?" He stopped short, looked up.

The sign over the porch front read, EGYPTIAN VIEW ARMS. BOARDING.

McCoy glanced at Cardiff, who stiffened. "*This* has got to be your digs. Let's see."

And before Cardiff could move, McCoy was up the front steps and inside the screen door.

Cardiff caught the door before it could slam and stepped in.

Silence. The obsequies over. The dear departed gone.

Even the parlor dust did not move, if there ever *had* been any dust. All the Tiffany lamps were dark and the flower vases empty. He heard McCoy in the kitchen and went to find him.

McCoy stood in front of the icebox, which was opened wide. There was no ice within, nor any cream or milk or butter and no drip pan under the box to be drunk by a thirsty dog after midnight. The pantry, similarly, displayed no leopard bananas or Ceylonese or Indian spices. A river of quiet wind had entered the house and left with the priceless stuffs.

McCoy muttered, scribbling, "That's enough evidence."

"Evidence?"

"Everyone's hiding. Everything's stashed. When I leave—bingo!—the grass gets cut, the icebox drips. How did they know I was *coming*? Now, I don't suppose there's a Western Union in this no-horse town?" He spied a telephone in the hallway, picked it up, listened. "No dial tone." He glanced through the screen door. "No postman in sight. I am in a big damn isolation booth."

McCoy ambled out to sit on the front porch glider, which squealed as if threatening to fall. McCoy read Cardiff's face.

"You look like a do-gooder," he said. "You run around saving people not worth saving. So what's so great about this town that's worth the Cardiff Salvation Army? That can't be the whole story. There's got to be a villain somewhere."

Cardiff held his breath.

McCoy pulled out his pad and scowled at it.

"I think I know the name of the villain," he muttered. "The Department of—"

He made Cardiff wait.

"—Highways?"

Cardiff exhaled.

"Bingo," McCoy whispered. "I see the headlines now: ACE REPORTER DEFENDS PERFECT TOWN FROM DESTRUCTION. Small type: Highway Bureau Insists on Pillage and Ruin. Next week: SUMMERTON SUES AND LOSES. Ace Reporter Drowns in Gin."

He shut his pad.

"Pretty good for an hour's work, yep?" he said.

"Pretty," said Cardiff.

Chapter 21

"This is gonna be great," said James Edward McCoy. "I can see it now: my byline on stories about how Summerton, Arizona, hit the rocks and sank. Johnstown flood stand aside. San Francisco earthquake, forget it. I'll expose how the government destroyed the innocents and plowed their front lawns with salt. First the *New York Times*, then papers in London, Paris, Moscow, even Canada. News junkies love to read about others' misery—here's an entire town being strangled to death by government greed. And I'm going to tell the world."

"Is that all you can see in this?" said Cardiff.

"Twenty-twenty vision!"

"Look around," said Cardiff. "It's a town with no people. No people, no story. Nobody cares if a town falls if there are no people in it. Your 'story' will run for one day, maybe. No book deal, no TV series, no film for you. Empty town. Empty bank account."

A scowl split McCoy's face.

"Son of a bitch," he murmured. "Where in hell is everyone?"

"They were never here."

"No one's here now, but the houses get painted, the lawns get mowed? They *were* just here, have to have been. You know that and you're lying to me. You know what's going on."

"I didn't till now."

"And you're not telling me? So you're keeping the headlines to yourself to protect this pathetic little ghost town?"

Cardiff nodded.

"Damn fool. Go on, stay poor and righteous. With you or without you I'm going to get to the bottom of this. Gangway!"

McCoy lunged down the porch steps, onto the street. He rushed up to the adjacent house and pulled open the door, stuck his head in, then entered. He emerged a moment later, slammed the door, and ran on to the next house, yanked open that screen door, jumped in, came out, his blood-red visage quoting dark psalms. Again and again he opened and closed the doors of half a dozen other empty houses.

Finally, McCoy returned to the front yard of the Egyptian View Arms. He stood there, panting, muttering to himself. As his voice drifted off into silence, a bird flew over and dropped a calling card on James Edward McCoy's vest.

Cardiff stared off across the meadow-desert. He imagined the shrieks of the arriving trainloads of hustling reporters. In his mind's eye he saw a twister of print inhaling the town and whirling it off into nothing.

"So." McCoy stood before him. "Where are all the people?"

"That seems to be a mystery," said Cardiff.

"I'm sending my first story now!"

"And how will you do that? No telegraphs or telephones."

"Holy jeez! How in hell do they *live*?"

"They're aerophiles, orchids, they breathe the air. But wait. You haven't examined everything. Before you go off half-cocked, there's one place I must show you."

Chapter 22

Cardiff led McCoy into the vast yard of motionless stones and flightless angels. McCoy peered at the markers.

"Damn. There's plenty of names, but no dates. When did they die?"

"They didn't," Cardiff said softly.

"Good God, lemme look closer."

McCoy took six steps west, four steps east, and came to . . .

The open grave with a coffin gaping wide, and a spade tossed to one side.

"What's this? Funeral today?"

"I dug that," said Cardiff. "I was looking for something."

"Something?" McCoy kicked some dirt clods into the grave. "You know more than you're telling. Why are you protecting this town?"

"All I know is that I might stay on."

"If you stay, you cannot tell these people the whole truth—that the bulldozers are coming, and the cement mixers, the funeral directors of progress. And *if* you leave, will you tell them *before* you go?"

Cardiff shook his head.

"Which leaves *me*," said McCoy, "as guardian of their virtues?"

"God, I hope not." Cardiff shifted by the open grave. Clods fell to drum the coffin.

McCoy backed off, nervously staring down at the open grave and into the empty coffin. "Hold on." A strange look came over his face. "My God, I bet you brought me here to stop my telephoning out, or even trying to leave town! You . . ."

At this, McCoy spun, lost his footing, and fell.

"Don't!" cried Cardiff.

McCoy fell into the coffin full-sprawled, eyes wide, to see the spade fall, loosened by accident or thrown in murder, he never knew. The spade struck his brow. The jolt shook the coffin lid. It slammed shut over his stunned and now colorless eyes.

The bang of the coffin lid shook the grave and knocked down dirt showers, smothering the box.

Cardiff stood amazed and in shock, a mile above.

Had McCoy slipped, he wondered, or was he *pushed*?

His foot dislodged another shower of dirt. Did he hear someone shrieking beneath the lid? Cardiff saw his shoes kick more dirt down into silence. With the box now hidden, he backed off, moaning, stared at the tombstone above etched with someone else's name, and thought, *That must be changed.*

And then he turned and ran, blindly, stumbling, out of the yard.

Chapter 23

I have committed murder, Cardiff thought.

No, no. McCoy buried himself. Slipped, fell, and shut the lid.

Cardiff walked almost backward down the middle of the street, unable to tear his gaze from the graveyard, as if expecting McCoy to appear, risen like Lazarus.

When he came to the Egyptian View Arms, he staggered up the walk and into the house, took a deep breath, and found his way to the kitchen.

Something fine was baking in the oven. A warm apricot pie lay on the pantry sill. There was a soft whisper under the icebox, where the dog was lapping the cool water in the summer heat. Cardiff backed off. *Like a crayfish,* he thought, *never forward.*

At the bay window he saw, on the vast lawn behind the house, two dozen bright blankets laid in a checkerboard with cutlery placed, empty plates waiting, crystal pitchers of lemonade, and wine, in preparation for a picnic. Outside he heard the soft drum of hooves.

Going out to the porch, Cardiff looked down at the curb. Claude, the polite and most intelligent horse, stood there, by the empty bread wagon.

Claude looked up at him.

"No bread to be delivered?" Cardiff called.

Claude stared at him with great moist brown eyes, and was silent.

"Would it be me that needs deliverance?" said Cardiff, as quiet as possible.

He walked down and stepped into the wagon.

Yes was the answer.

Claude started up and carried him through the town.

Chapter 24

They were passing the graveyard.

I have committed murder, Cardiff thought.

And, impulsively, he cried, "Claude!"

Claude froze and Cardiff jumped out of the wagon and rushed into the graveyard.

Swaying over the grave, he reached down in a terrible panic to lift the lid.

McCoy was there, not dead but sleeping, having given up, and was now taking a snooze.

Exhaling, Cardiff spoke down at his terrible enemy, glad that he was alive.

"Stay there," he said. "You don't know it, but you're going home." He dropped the lid gently, taking care to insert a twig in the gap between top and bottom to allow for air.

He ran back to Claude, who, sensing the visit was over, started off again at a good clop.

All around them the yards and porches were empty.

Where, Cardiff wondered, *has everyone gone?*

He had his answer when Claude stopped.

They stood before a large, rather handsome brick building, its entrance flanked by two Egyptian sphinxes lying supine, half-lioness and half-god, with faces he could almost name.

Cardiff read these words: HOPE MEMORIAL LIBRARY.

And in small letters beneath that: KNOW HOPE, ALL YE WHO ENTER HERE.

He climbed the library steps to find Elias Culpepper standing before the great double front doors. Culpepper behaved as if he'd been expecting the younger man, and motioned at him to sit down on the library steps.

"We've been waiting for you," he said.

"We?" said Cardiff.

"The whole town, or most of it," said Culpepper. "Where have you been?"

"The graveyard," said Cardiff.

"You spend too much time there. Is there a problem?"

"Not anymore, if you can help me mail something home. Is there a train expected anytime soon?"

"Should be one passing through sometime today," said Elias Culpepper. "Doubt it'll stop. That hasn't happened in . . ."

"*Can* it be stopped?"

"Could try flares."

"I've got a package I want sent, if you can stop it."

"I'll light the flares," said Culpepper. "Where's this package going?"

"Home," Cardiff said again. "Chicago."

He wrote a name and address on a page ripped from his notepad, and handed the piece of paper to Culpepper.

"Consider it done," said Culpepper. He rose and said, "Now I think you ought to go inside."

Cardiff turned and pushed the great library doors and stepped in.

He read a sign above the front counter: CARPE DIEM. SEIZE THE DAY. It could have also read: SEIZE A BOOK. FIND A LIFE. BIRTH A METAPHOR.

His gaze drifted to find a large part of the town's population seated at two dozen tables, books open, reading, and keeping the SILENCE that other signs suggested.

As if pulled by a single string, they turned, nodded at Cardiff, and turned back to their books.

The young woman behind the library front desk was an incredible beauty.

"My God," he whispered. "Nef!"

She raised her hand and pointed, then beckoned for him to follow.

She walked ahead of him and she might well have had a lantern in her hand to light the dim stacks, for her face was illumination. Wherever she glanced, the darkness failed and a faint light touched the gold lettering along the shelves.

The first stack was labeled: ALEXANDRIA ONE.

And the second: ALEXANDRIA TWO.

And the last: ALEXANDRIA THREE.

"Don't say it," he said, quietly. "Let me. The libraries at Alexandria, five hundred or a thousand years before Christ, had three fires, maybe more, and everything burned."

"Yes," Nef said. "This first stack contains all or most of the books burned in the first fire, an accident.

"This second stack from the second burning, also an accident, has all the lost books and destroyed texts of that terrible year.

"And the last, the third, contains all the books from the third conflagration—a burning by mobs, the purposeful destruction of history, art, poetry, and plays in 455 B.C.

"In 455 B.C.," she repeated quietly.

"My God," he said, "how were they all saved, how did they get *here*?"

"We *brought* them."

"How?!"

"We are tomb robbers." Nef ran her finger along the stacks. "For the profit of the mind, the extension of the soul, whatever the soul is. We can only try to describe the mystery. Long before Schliemann, who found not one but twenty Troys, our ancestors played finders-keepers with the grandest library in time, one that would never burn, would live forever and allow those who entered to touch and scan, a chance to run after an extra piece of existence. This building is absolute proof against fire. In one form or another, it has traveled from Moses, Caesar, Christ, and will continue on toward the new Apollo and the Moon that the rocket chariot will reach."

"But still," he said. "Those libraries were ruined. Are these duplicates of duplicates? The lost are found, but how?"

Nef laughed quietly. "It was a hard task. Down through the centuries, a book here or there, a play one place, a poem another. A huge jigsaw, fitted in pieces."

She moved on in the comfortable twilight spilling through the library's tall windows, brushing her fingers over the names and titles.

"Remember when Hemingway's wife left his novel manuscript on a train, lost forever?"

"Did he divorce or kill her?"

"The marriage survived for a while. But that manuscript is here."

He looked at the worn typewriter box labeled: FOOTHILLS; KILIMANJARO.

"Have you read it?"

"We're afraid to. If it is as fine as some of his work, it would break our hearts because it must remain lost. If it's bad, we might feel worse. Perhaps Papa knew it was best for it to remain lost. He wrote another *Kilimanjaro,* with *Snows* instead."

"How in hell did you find it?"

"The week it was lost we advertised. Which is more than Papa did. We sent him a copy. He never replied, and the *Snows* was published a year later."

Again she moved to touch more volumes.

"Edgar Allan Poe's final poem, rejected. Herman Melville's last tale, unseen."

"How?"

"We visited their deathbeds in their last hours. The dying sometimes speak in tongues. If you know the language of deliriums you can transcribe their strange sad truths. We tend them like special guardians late at night, and summon a last vital spark and listen closely and keep their words. Why? Since we are the passengers of time, we thought it only proper to save what might be saved on our passage to eternity, to preserve what might be lost if neglected, and add some small bit of our far-traveling and long life. We have guarded not only Troy and its ruins and sifted the Egyptian sands for wise stones to put beneath our tongues to clear our speech, but we have, like cats, inhaled the breaths of mortals, siphoned and published their whispers. Since we have been gifted with long lives, the least we can do is pass that gift on in inanimate objects—novels, poems, plays—books that rouse to life when scanned by a living eye. You must never receive a gift, ever, without returning the gift twice over. From Jesus of Nazareth to noon tomorrow, our baggage is the library and its silent speech. Each book is Lazarus, yes? And you the reader, by opening the covers, bid Lazarus to come forth. And he lives again, *it* lives again, the dead words warmed by your glance."

"I never thought . . .," Cardiff said.

"Think." She smiled. "Now," she said, "I believe it's time for a picnic, to celebrate we don't know what. But celebrate we must."

Chapter 25

The picnic was spread waiting on the back lawn of the EGYPTIAN VIEW ARMS.

"Speech!" someone called.

"I don't know how to begin," Cardiff said.

"At the beginning!" There was a gentle laughter.

Cardiff took a deep breath and plunged in.

"As you may know, the State Department of Highways has been measuring string from Phoenix east and north and from Gallup north and west. The exact measurements of a new freeway will touch latitude 89 eighty miles west of longitude 40."

Someone on the far side of the picnic let his sandwich fall and cried, "My God, that's *us*!"

"No!" someone else cried, and a dozen others whispered, "No!"

"That's not possible," someone said.

"Anything," said Cardiff, quietly, "in government, is possible."

"They can't *do* that," one of the ladies cried.

"But they can. No freeway in any part of your state has ever been put on the ballot. The highway men, God listen to that, *highway* men, are their own conscience."

"And you traveled here to warn us?" said Elias Culpepper.

Cardiff blushed. "No."

"You were going to keep it secret!?"

"I wanted to see your town. I planned nothing. I assumed you all knew."

"We know nothing," said Elias Culpepper. "God almighty. You might as well say Vesuvius is threatening to erupt at our city limits!"

"I must admit," said Cardiff, "that when I saw your faces, had breakfast, lunch, and dinner with you, I knew I couldn't leave and not tell you."

"Tell us again," said Elias Culpepper.

Cardiff looked at Nef, who gave him the merest nod.

"The State Highway Commission . . ."

Lightning struck. Earthquakes shook. A comet hit the Earth. Cats leaped off roofs. Dogs bit their tails and died.

And the picnic ground, the sweet grass, was empty.

Sweet Jesus, thought Cardiff, *have* I *done this?*

"Fool, idiot, stupid dumb idiot fool," he muttered.

He opened his eyes and saw Nef standing on a rise of green lawn calling over to him. "Come into the shade. You'll die of sunstroke."

And he went over into the shade.

Chapter 26

My *God,* Cardiff thought, *even the sunflowers have turned away.* He could not see their faces, but he was certain they fixed him with a fiery stare.

"I'm empty," he said at last. "I've told all my secrets. Now, Nef, you must give me yours."

"Well," she said, and began to take sandwiches out of a hamper, to cut bread and butter it and offer it to him as she spoke.

"Everyone in this town was once somewhere else," she said. "We came together one by one. Long, long ago, we knocked elbows in Rome or Paris or Athens or Dallas or Portland until, very late in time, we found out that there was a place where we might collect. Sanctuary, Arizona, was one of the names, but that was foolish. I imagine Summerton's just as foolish, but it fits. It has to do with flowers and survival. We all grew up in Madrid or Dublin or Milwaukee, some in France or Italy. In the very beginning, a long time ago, there were some children, but as time passed the children got fewer. It had nothing to do with wine or flowers, nothing to do with the environment or the families, even though it seems to have been genetic. I guess you'd call us 'sports.' That's a scientific term for something that can't be explained. The Darwinians said the process was all jumps, hops, genetic leaps, with no links between. Suddenly, members of a family whose ancestors had lived to seventy years were living to ninety, a hundred. Others, even longer. But the peculiar thing, of course, was that there were those of us—young men and women—who did not much change at all, and then simply did *not* change. While all our friends moved on to sickness and old age, we strange ones stayed behind. It was one long picnic spread over the entire North American continent and Europe. And we, the lonely ones, were the exceptions to the rule of 'Grow up, grow old, and certainly die.' For a while, we hardly noticed this peculiar longevity ourselves, except to note that we felt fine and looked good while our friends jumped headlong into the grave. We peculiars lingered in mid-spring with summer always just around the corner, and autumn somewhere far down the road, not even a rumor. Does any of this make sense?"

Cardiff nodded, fascinated with what she was saying, the flow and beauty of her telling making it, somehow, believable.

"Most of our meetings were by chance," she went on. "A trip on a ferry boat, a voyage on a ship, a descent in an elevator, a collision going through doors, a place at a table, a passing glance on a seventeenth-century street, but somewhere in time we gave pause and asked where we came from, what we were doing, and how old were we, and saw the lie in each other's faces.

"'I am twenty, I am twenty-two, I am thirty,' we said, at tea, or drinking in a bar, but the truth was not there. We had been born during Victoria's reign, or when Lincoln was shot, or as Henry VIII laid his queen's head on the chopping block. It took many years for the truth to rise, one here, two there, until our real births were revealed. 'Good Lord,' we cried. 'We are Time's twins. You ninety-five, yes, and I one hundred and ten.' And we searched each other's face, as in mirrors, and saw soft-showered April and sun-filled May instead of raining October, dark November, and Christmas with no lights. We wept. And when the weeping stopped we compared long-lost child-hoods and the bullies who had tormented us for being different, and not knowing why. Friends abandoned us when suddenly the friends were fifty and sixty and we still looked fresh out of high school. Marriages failed and the grave shut out all the rest. And we were left stranded in a great mausoleum that echoed with the laughter of school chums now incinerated or, if still alive, wielding crutches and piloting wheelchairs. Soon we found, by instinct, that it was best to keep moving, on to new towns to take up new lives, old souls in new bodies, lying about our past. We were not happy, then. We *became* happy. How? The rumor, after centuries, of a new town reached us. The myth held that a man on horseback crossing a great desert got off in emptiness, built a hut, and waited for others to arrive. He placed an ad in a magazine that extolled the *young* weather, *fresh* times, *new* circumstances. It contained multitudinous hints that might be unraveled by similar freaks in Oswego and Peoria, fellow lonely ones who watched the fall of friends all around and heard the earth thunder on too many coffin lids. They felt their limbs, still as limber as on graduation day, and wondered about their desolation. They read and reread the strange travel ad that promised a haven, a new place, as yet unnamed. A town that was small, but growing. *Only* twenty-one-year-olds need apply. Well, there, you see? Hints! No direct pronouncements. But lonelies everywhere, from

Deadfall, Dakota, and Wintershade, England, felt the hair rise on their necks and packed their bags. Maybe, they thought, it would be worth the time and travel. And what was once a roadside bypass became a post office, a Pony Express standby, and then a jerkwater train stop, where strangers scanned each other's faces and found yesterday's sunrise instead of tomorrow's midnight. They were driven by more than birthright. They were driven by one final terrible fact: at last, none could give or produce children."

"It came to that?" whispered Cardiff.

"Yes, it finally happened. We lived longer but at a price. We had to be our own children, having none. So, year by year, strangers got off the train, one way, or rode up on horseback or walked the long walk and never looked back. By 1900 Summerton had its crops planted, its gardens full, its gazebos built, its social life established, and world communications running out but not in. No radios, no TVs, no newspapers, well, almost none. There was and is the *Culpepper Summerton News*, with not much news, for no one was born and almost no one died. Occasionally someone fell down a flight of stairs, or off a ladder, but we tend to mend fast. No cars, so no fatalities. But we were all busy, busy raising food, socializing, writing, dreaming. And then, of course, there were romances. For while we could not propagate, we could still enact passion. A perfect population, assembled from the four corners of creation, a jigsaw beautifully fitted with no rough edges. Everyone had a job, some wrote poems, others novels, all got published in far places, fantasies mainly of cities beyond belief, whose readers thought the tales mere figments of wild imagination, but *we* were *living* it. So there it is. *Here* it is. Perfect weather, perfect town, perfect lives. Long lives. Most of us shook hands with Lincoln, attended the obsequies at Grant's tomb, and now . . ."

"Now?" said Cardiff.

"You are a messenger of doom, come to destroy it all."

"I am not the message, Nef. I do deliver it, yes."

"I know," said Nef, quietly. "But how I wish you could go off and come back with some better truth."

"If I could, so help me God, Nef, I'd gladly bring it to you."

"Go," she said. "Please. Find it and bring it here."

But he could only sit on the evergreen grass of eternal summer and let the tears run down his cheeks.

Chapter 27

"And now," said Nef.

"Now?" said Cardiff.

"I must prove that I do not wish to kill the bearer of bad news. Come."

And she led him across the lawn where the picnic blankets still lay as after a storm, tossed and half-furled, and some few dogs had arrived with the army ants while several cats waited for the beasts to leave, and Nef walked among them and opened the front door of the Egyptian View Arms and, ducking his head, blushing, Cardiff stepped in swiftly, but she was already at the stairs and halfway up before he touched the first riser, and then they were in her tower room and he looked and saw that her vast bed had been stripped and the windows thrown open wide with their wind-tossed curtains and the town clock was striking four in the afternoon as Nef lifted her arms and a great soft bloom of sheet rose in a summer cloud over the bed and he seized his half and with her gentled it down in a field of white over the bed to cover its face. And they stood back and watched the late afternoon exhale and fill the lace and blow the curtains inward toward the bed, like a fall of never-arriving snow, and there was a glass of lemonade on either bedside table, and his questioning look caused her to laugh and shake her head. Only lemonade, nothing more.

"Because," she said, "*I* will inebriate you."

It was a long fall to the bed. She arrived an eternity later. He sank under white sheets of snow and recalled his whole life, in a whiplash of memory.

"Say it," he heard her cry, a long way off.

"Oh, Nef, Nef," he cried. "I love you!"

It was twilight. The lace curtains continued to move in a white snowfall above them. The Chinese wind crystals on the porch chimed. They lay hand in hand, dear chums most dearly met, eyes shut, drinking the silence, dressed only by the late sunlight and the weather, and at last she said: "How would you like to live a few hundred years? Or," she added, "forever, whichever comes first."

"Forever, I think," he said.

"Good." Her hand tightened on his. "Trust me?"

"Yes. No. Yes."

"Which?"

"I'm confused," he said. "I'm not one of your miraculous longtime historical 'sports.' Can you make me one?"

"You *came* to us, remember."

"But for two reasons. To see your town before it was buried under cement. *And* I was carrying the news of your destruction, which you didn't know, and I had to tell. Two reasons."

"Three," she said. "There was a sense in you, as in most of us, like a homing pigeon, a thing printed in your blood or behind your face, a ghost in your head. And why not? A ghost of a need, just as our ghosts moved us, let us recognize each other when we met on street corners or in passing trains. Your third reason for coming here was as natural as breathing. You came here looking for the right place, but you couldn't admit it, so you gave other reasons. You're like us, or almost like us. You have the inclination, the grammar printed in your genes, to let you live to four times the age you are now. We can only encourage you with our company and, of course, the weather, food, and wine."

"*Is* the fountain of youth bottled, then?"

"No, no." She laughed quietly. "There is no such medicine, no cure. We only supplement what God gave you first. Some people never have colds, never break bones, don't get headaches, drink without getting hangovers, climb mountains without having to stop to rest, remain passionate beyond belief, all God-given. Our gift from Darwin's God or God's Darwin is simply being part of a moveable feast of inheritance moving upstream against death. Oh, Lord." She laughed quietly. "How can moveable feasts swim upstream? But you know my meaning. You refuse that dark tide that sinks down into night. Otherwise you would not be here, listening to a fool."

"Beloved fool, crazed lady, beautiful lunatic," he murmured.

"Now, let me give you the final explanation for myself and all the friends whom you have met here. The great 'medicine' was finding that we were alive and loving it. We have celebrated every day of our lives. The celebration, the exhilaration, of worshipping the gift, has kept us young. Does that sound impossible? By simply knowing you're alive and looking at the sun and enjoying the weather and speaking it every moment of your existence, *this* ensures our longevity. We live every moment of our existence to the fullest, and *that* is a superb medicine. In that way we refuse the darkness. Now think of what I've said and tell me about your future."

He lay back and scanned the ceiling for answers. "Good grief!" he said. "I don't know. I've got obligations back home. Many friends. Mother and father both still alive. A woman I've been almost engaged to for two years—two years—think about it! I've been dragging my feet, taking advantage, typical male. So many loose ends, knots to be tied, goodbyes to be said. I've just *started* thinking and don't know what to think. I know that I love this town, these people, and you. God, I'm in the midst of love and am afraid to fall further. It's too much in a few days."

She waited and saw an outline of her future on the ceiling, also. "I will not be the cat on your chest that inhales the air you need to breathe," she said. "But you must decide. And I have saved one final thing for last. If you stay you will be in many ways the center of our existence. You will definitely be the center of mine. Because, as you well know, there have been no children born in this town for a long, long while."

"And soon," he put in at last, "the first new child must be born and someone must be the father. Perhaps that father is me."

"Perhaps you already are." She placed her hands upon her stomach, as if trying to sense a presence. "Perhaps you are."

"That would be quite a responsibility," he said.

"So," she said, "I've put a big burden on you. I must let you go and hope that you will return. But you must decide soon. We won't be here much longer, soon the town will be gone. We're leaving."

"Is that possible?"

"Yes. It's happened many times before, before Summerton even existed. We carry our homes in our heads. All across country, from Providence to Kansas to points farther west. If we can't save this town, we'll burn it and scatter the ashes. We won't be revealed again. The bullies must never know we exist."

"Oh God," he whispered. "It is a burden. Let me sleep. Sometimes in dreams I find answers."

"Sleep then," she said.

"You," he said. "Not the weather, not the genetics, you, dear Nef," he paused, "are my fountain of youth."

"Let me make you young again," she said.

And sealed his mouth with hers.

Chapter 28

He slept and he dreamed.

He was on the train, going east, and then suddenly he was in Chicago, and even more suddenly, he was in front of the Art Institute and was going up the stairs and through the corridors to stand before the great *Sunday in the Park* painting.

A woman was standing by the painting and she turned and it was his fiancée.

As he watched, she grew older, aging before his eyes, and she said to him, "You've changed."

He said, "No, I haven't changed at all."

"Your face is different. You've come to say goodbye."

"No, just to see how you are," he said.

"No, you've come to say goodbye."

And as he watched, she grew even older and he felt very small, standing in front of the painting and trying to think of something to say.

Quite suddenly she was gone.

He walked out of the building and there at the bottom of the stairs were seven or eight of his friends.

As he watched, they grew older and they said the same things that she had said.

"You've come to say goodbye."

"No," he insisted. "No, I haven't done that."

Then he turned and ran back into the building, a young man suddenly old among old paintings.

And then he awoke.

Chapter 29

He sat for a long while listening to the wind howl in the chimney and the rain funnels outside.

The old house creaked down into a deep swell of night then backed up and over, out of sight of land and light.

Rats practiced graffiti on the walls and spiders played harps so high that only the hairs inside his ears heard and quivered.

How much loss, how much gain? he wondered. *How much leave, and how much remain?*

What to decide? he thought.

All right, he called into himself. *What? Which?*

Not a stir of dark in his head. Not an echo.

Just a whisper: *Sleep.*

And he slept again and put out the light behind his eyes.

He heard a locomotive whistle across his dreams.

The train was gliding, rushing in the night, taking the curves under the moon, hitting the long straightaways, tossing dust, scattering sparks, laying out echoes, and he was atilt and adream and somehow the familiar words came back in his head:

One kiss and all time's your dominion
One touch and no death can be cold.
One night puts off graveyard opinion
One hour and you'll never grow old.
Drink deep of the wine of forever
Drink long of eternity's stuff
Where everyman's learned and clever,
And two billion loves not enough.

He cried out in his dream. *No!* And then again, *Oh God, yes.*

And some final few words spelled his dreams:

Somewhere a band is playing,
Playing the strangest tunes,
Of sunflower seeds and sailors,
Who tide with the strangest moons.

He was waking now. His mouth sighed:

Somewhere a band is playing
Listen, O, listen, that tune?
Learn it and you'll dance on forever
In June and yet June and more . . . June.

The train was not far off now. It was rounding some hills. The sun was rising and he knew he had changed his mind.

He looked out at a sunrise that was bloody, a town filled with farewell light, and a weather that was so strange he would not forget it for a thousand days.

He saw his face in the bathroom mirror as he shaved, and the eyes looked immensely sad.

He came down to breakfast and sat before the mound of hotcakes and did not eat.

Nef, across from him, saw what he had seen in the mirror and sat back in her chair.

"Have you been thinking?" she asked.

He took a deep breath. Up to this very moment he didn't know what would come from his mouth.

"Stay," she said, before he could speak.

"I wish that I could."

"Stay."

And here she reached and took his hand.

And it was a warm hand and his own was cold. She seemed a goddess, bending to reach into his tomb and help him out.

"Please."

"Oh God," he cried. "Oh Christ, let me be!" He wept inside. "You don't understand. I'm not made to *not* grow old."

"How can you know?"

"Each of us knows. I was born to live and die at seventy. Then I will really be filled up. The fire of life, the good stuff, goes straight up the chimney. The sins, the sadness, whatever, stays like soot on the chimney walls. One can gather only so much darkness. I've collected too much. How do you knock the soot off the walls inside your soul?"

"With a chimney sweep," she said. "Let me sweep and knock those walls until you laugh. I can, if you let me."

"I won't allow it."

"No," she said, quietly. "I don't suppose you can. Oh, God, I might cry now. But I won't. Goodbye."

"I'm not going yet."

"But I am. I can't watch you go. Come back someday."

"Do you think I'll never come back?"

She nodded, eyes shut.

"I'm sorry," he said. "It's so hard. I don't know if I'm ready to live a hundred and thirty years. I wonder if anyone is or can be. It's just," he said, "it sounds so . . . lonely. Leaving everyone behind. Coming to the day when the last friend goes into the graveyard."

"You'll make new friends."

"Yes, but there are no friends like the old ones. You can't replace them."

"No. You can't."

She looked at the door.

"If you go, and you do decide to come back, to try and find us, don't wait too long."

"Or it won't work? I know. I'll be too old. Must I decide before I'm . . . fifty?"

"Just come back to us," she said.

And suddenly her chair was empty.

Chapter 30

At the train station, there were sunflowers out on the track. Someone had been there ahead of him and if it was Elias Culpepper, he never knew.

The train stopped this time, and he got on and as he bought a ticket from the conductor he asked, "Do you remember me?"

The man looked at his face intently, scowled, and looked again and said, "Can't say I do."

And the train gathered steam and chugged away from the station and Summerton, Arizona, was left behind.

Chapter 31

The train flew across flat corn lands, over the horizon, by the lake and to the great turbulent city next to the lake, and he was running up the steps of the museum and walking among paintings to sit before the endlessly intriguing Seurat, where the Sunday strollers stood still in an eternal park.

Now beside him sat Laura, glancing back and forth from the green park to him, stunned and questioning.

At last she said, "What have you done to your face?"

"My face?" he said.

"It's changed," she said.

"I didn't change it."

"What is it, then?"

"Things. Things changed it."

"Can you change it back?"

"I'll try."

And then, as in the dream, but now in reality, he walked down the steps of the museum and all of his friends were waiting at the bottom of the stairs.

There were Tom and Pete and Will and Sam and all the rest and they said, "Let's go out for a long dinner."

He said, "No, I haven't the time."

"You've only just said hello," they said.

"It's not easy," he said. "I've known you all for years. But, *I've* changed. And now I've got to go."

He looked back up and at the top of the stairs stood Laura. A single tear rolled down her cheek as she stared at his so-familiar yet oh-so-changed face.

He smiled, and turned away and walked down the street toward the railroad station.

Chapter 32

The train came out of the east and without thinking of time or place, glided slowly past a spot that was marked only by dust, wind, cacti, a scatter of leaves, and a profusion of ticket-punch confetti that celebrated on the air and settled when the train was gone.

Meanwhile, a familiar suitcase skidded to a halt on the remains of a ramshackle station platform, a few surfboards on a tide of sand, followed by a man in a wrinkled summer suit who tumbled out like an acrobat, shouting with pride when he landed, swaying but intact.

"Damn, I *did* it!"

He picked up his flimsy suitcase and stared around at desolation, wiped his brow, and looked toward the end of the station platform where the mail catcher stood. He saw a white envelope in its steel holding arm and went to pluck it from the equipment's grasp. On the front of the envelope he saw his name. He looked around, studying thirty thousand acres of blowing dust, and no roads leading in or out of the desolation.

"Well," he whispered, "I've returned. So . . ."

He opened the envelope and read:

"My dear James. So you've come back. You had to! A lot has happened since you went away."

He paused and regarded the empty desert where Summerton, Arizona, once had stood.

He returned to the letter:

"When you read this, we will be gone. There will be nothing left but sand and a few footprints soon to be blown away by the wind. We did not wait for the arrival of the machines and their operators. We pulled up our roots and vanished. Have you heard of those orchards that once thrived near certain small California towns? As the small towns grew into big cities, the orange trees mysteriously disappeared. And yet, passing motorists who glance off toward the mountains will see that somehow those orchards have drifted or blown to settle and take root in the foothills, green and flourishing, far from the gasoline stampede.

"Well, my dear James, that is us. We are like those orchards. We've heard, through the years, late in the night, the great boa constrictor, the terrible endless snake of concrete rushing upon us, nearly soundless, no men swearing or shouting or revving tractor and truck engines, but just a terrible oiled hiss, the sound of reptiles sidewinding the grass or sifting the sand, all by itself, no men guiding, no one riding its loops and folds, a destination to itself, mindless but drawn by body warmth, the heat of people. And so, drawn by that warmth, as reptiles are, it came seeking to disturb our sleep, evict us from our homes. All this we imagined in our dreams, long before you arrived with your awful burden of news. So do not let this weigh too heavily on your soul. We already knew this day was coming; it was only a matter of time.

"Years back, dear James, we began to prepare for the death of our town and the exodus of our people. We brought in hundreds of giant wooden wheels and a plentiful supply of heavy timbers and iron fastenings to bind them together. The wheels lay waiting on the edge of town for years along with the timbers drying in the sun.

"And then the deadfall trumpet blew, to tell it with your humor, at the picnic of the Apocalypse

and you saw the faces before you pale with each new revelation. Once in mid-speech I thought you might back off, break, and run, panicked by our panic. Yet you stayed on. Finished, I thought you might fall and die so you could not witness our deaths.

"And when you looked up we were gone.

"We knew you were sick at heart, so I gave you what medicine I had, my attention and my pitiful words. And when you left on the noon train, leaping on long before it stopped, we looked at all those iron and wooden wheels beyond the city, and the platform timbers on which we imagined our houses, barns, and orchards transported so far off that no one would suspect this place had once known a life and now would know no more.

"You have seen, have you not, those solitary parades, single houses hoisted up on wooden plates and pulled like toys along the streets to empty lots to be replanted while the old sites turned to dust? Multiply that by three hundred homes and witness a parade of pachyderms, an entire town gliding toward the foothills, followed by the orchard trees.

"It is all quite impossible. Yet, in times of war, think of the preparations, the blueprints, the final accomplishments, thousands of ships, tens of thousands of tanks and guns, more tens of thousands of

rifles, bullets, millions of iron helmets, tens of millions of shirts and jackets. How complicated but how necessary when war shouted and we ran. How much simpler our task to uproot a town, to run and rebirth it with wheels.

"In time, our fevers turned into a festival of triumph instead of a funeral march. We were forced on by the imagined thunder, the threatening hiss, of that new road beyond the eastern range. At night we could hear the road coming toward us full steam, rushing to catch us before we vanished.

"Well, the purveyors of concrete and movers of earth did not catch us. On the final day of our escape there remained, where you stand, the ruined station surrounded by a jungle of orange and lemon trees. These were the last to go, a beautiful excursion of softly scented orchards that drifted, four abreast, across the desert to nourish our newly hidden town.

"There you have it, dear James. We moved and left no pebble, no stone, no basement larder, no graveyard tombstone. All, all, all of it was transported.

"And when the highway arrives, what will they find? Was there ever a Summerton, Arizona, a courthouse, a town hall, a picnic ground, an empty school? No, never. Look to the dust.

"I will post this letter on the station platform mail-loop in the hope that it will reach you, if you should return. Somehow I know you will come back. I can feel your touch on this envelope even as I sign and seal it.

"When you finish reading this, dear friend and lover, consign it to the weather."

And below this was her signature: Nef.

He tore the letter in quarters and then quarters of quarters, and quarters again, and loosed the confetti into the air.

Now, he thought, *which way?*

He squinted at the northern rim of desert where lay a length of low half-green hills. He imagined the orchards.

There, he thought.

He had taken but one step when he looked back.

Like an old brown dog, his suitcase lay on the dust-blown station platform.

No, he thought, *you're another time.*

The luggage lay, waiting.

"Stay," he said.

The luggage stayed.

He walked on.

Chapter 33

It was twilight when he reached the first row of orange trees.

It was deepening twilight when he saw the familiar crowds of sunflowers in each yard and the sign, EGYPTIAN VIEW ARMS, swaying above the verandah.

The sun was almost gone as he walked up the last sidewalk, mounted the porch steps, stood before the screen door, and pressed the doorbell. It chimed quietly. A slender shadow appeared on the hall stair.

"Nef," he said at last, quietly.

"Nef," he said, "I'm home."

Leviathan '99

"Radio Dream"

In 1939, when I was nineteen, I fell in love with the radio dramas of Norman Corwin.

I met him later, when I was twenty-seven, and he encouraged me to write my Martian stories, thus causing *The Martian Chronicles* to be born.

Along through the years my dream was to one day have Norman Corwin direct one of my radio dramas.

When I returned from my year in Ireland, after writing the screenplay for John Huston's *Moby Dick,* I was still deeply under the influence of Herman Melville and his leviathan whale. Simultaneously I was still under the spell of Shakespeare, who had entered my life when I was in high school.

After I'd been home from Ireland for a while, I began to consider taking the Melville mythology and placing it in outer space.

NBC had recently encouraged Norman Corwin and me to collaborate on a one-hour radio drama. When I finished my first script of *Leviathan '99*, about spaceships instead of sailing ships, mad astronaut captains instead of seafaring captains, and the blinding white comet replacing the great white whale, I turned in the script to Norman, who then sent it on to NBC.

At that time television was increasing in popularity, diminishing radio, and NBC responded to my script by saying, "Can you break this down into three-minute segments, which we can broadcast over a period of days?"

Stunned, Norman and I withdrew the script and I sent it to BBC Radio in London, who produced it, with Christopher Lee playing the lead of the insane captain of the spaceship *Cetus*.

The radio production was excellent, but of course my dream of having something produced and directed for radio by Corwin still remained unborn. Suffering from what I now call my "delusions of Shakespeare," I dared to double the length of my *Leviathan '99* script and staged it as a play at a Samuel Goldwyn studio soundstage in the spring of 1972. Unfortunately, adding an additional forty pages to the script destroyed my original intent. The essential story was lost. The critics' reviews were unanimous in their vitriol.

In the years that followed I produced *Leviathan '99* here and there, gradually whittling away extraneous pages in an attempt to get it back somewhere near the original one-hour version done for radio.

Thirty years later this novella is my final effort to focus and revitalize what began as a radio dream for Norman Corwin. Whether or not it deserves to appear in this incarnation is for you to decide.

DEDICATED WITH

GREAT ADMIRATION

to Herman Melville

Chapter 1

Call me Ishmael.

Ishmael? In this year 2099 when strange new ships head beyond the stars instead of merely toward them? Attack the stars instead of fearing them? A name like Ishmael?

Yes.

My parents flew with the first brave ones to Mars. Turned less than brave, gone sick for Earth, they returned home. Conceived on that journey, I was born in space.

My father knew his Bible and recalled another outcast who wandered dead seas long years before Christ.

And I being, at that time, the only child fleshed and delivered forth in space, how better to name me than as my father did.

And he did indeed call me . . . Ishmael.

Some years ago I thought I would ride all the seas of wind that roam this world. Whenever it is a damp November in my soul, I know it is high time to brave the skies again.

So I soared up among bird cries, bright kites, and thunderheads on a Saturday, late summer in this year of 2099, borne upon my own jet-packet power. I flew over and away toward Cape Kennedy in my wild journey hung upon the air, a fledgling bird among the memories of old da Vinci's antique aircraft dreams. I was warmed by the real fire of great birds of steel, and felt the floodgates of the vast and waiting universe swing open my soul.

There were great concussions at a distance: the furnace heat of Kennedy and its thousands of rockets, burning in towers all about. When the fires died at last, only a simple wind whispered.

Then, quickly and calmly, I descended into town, where a river flowed for me to walk upon, a moving sidewalk.

Shadows stirred all about me as I glided through architectural arches and doors. Where was I going? Not to a cold metal barracks for tired spacemen, no, but a beautiful, quietly programmed, machined Garden of Eden. I was to attend an academy for astronauts to train for a great voyage beyond the stars, a mission about which as of yet I knew nothing.

Such a place is a world between: part meadow for mind, part gymnasium for flesh, and part theological seminary, reaching ever skyward in its thoughts. For does space not have the look of a vast cathedral?

So I walked among shifting shadows and entered the reception foyer of the school's dormitory. I registered by pressing my hand to an identity panel, which read my sweaty prints like some modern witch of palmistry, and instantaneously chose my roommate for my coming mission.

There was a buzz, a hum, a bell, and a voice—female, sibilant, mechanical—came from somewhere above: "Ishmael Hunnicut Jones; twenty-nine years; height, five-foot-ten; eyes, blue; hair, brown; bone frame, light. Please attend: floor one, room nine. Cubicle roommate, Quell."

And I repeated, "Quell."

"Quell?" another voice cried behind me. "My God, that's terrible."

Yet another voice added, "God help you, Mr. Jones."

I turned to find three astronauts of varying sizes and demeanors, all some years older than me, facing me, holding drinks. One was held out to me.

"Take this, Ishmael Jones," said the first man, who was tall and thin. "You'll need it if you're going upstairs to meet that monster," he said. "Drink up."

"But first," said the second, holding out his hand to stay my arm, "how do you fly, shallow or deep?"

"Why, deep, I think," I said. "Deep space."

"By the timid mile or the great light-year?"

"Light-year, yes," I thought, then said.

"You may drink with us, then."

The third man, who had been silent to this point, spoke up. "I'm John Redleigh. This fellow here," with a nod toward the tall man, "is Sam Small. And he," indicating the remaining man, "is Jim Downs."

And so we drank. Small declared, "We give you permission to share our space, and also with God's permission. Do you go to unravel a comet's tail?"

"I think I do."

"Have you searched for comets before?"

"Now's my time."

"Well said. Look there."

The three men turned and nodded toward a vast video screen across the reception hall. As if aware of our regard, it pulsed to life, and displayed an immense photo of a blinding white comet pulling planets in its wake.

"The lovely destroyer of the universe," said Small. "The eater of the sun."

"Can comets do that?" I asked.

"That, and more. *Especially* that one."

Downs said, "Why, if God should manifest here, He'd come as a comet. Are you one for jumping down the throat of such a holy presence, boy, and dancing in its bright guts?"

"I am," I said, reluctantly, "if it should be absolutely inescapable."

"Then let's drink to him, aye, men? Let's drink to young Ishmael Hunnicut Jones."

At which moment I heard a faint electronic buzz, a pulse, at some distance. I listened, and the buzz grew louder with each pulse, as if it was coming nearer.

"That," I said. "What's that?"

"That?" said Redleigh. "That sound like a scourge of locusts in flight?"

I nodded.

"A scourge of locusts?" said Small. "That's a fine way to refer to our captain."

"Captain?" I said. "Who is he?"

Redleigh said, "Let it be for now, Mr. Jones. You'd best get to your room and meet up with Quell. My God, yes, go meet Quell."

"From beyond the great Andromeda Nebula, he is," Downs said, in a confidential tone. "Tall, huge, immense, and . . ."

"A spider," the first mate interjected.

"Yes, yes," Downs continued. "A vast, tall, giant green spider."

"But . . .," said Small, frowning slightly at his companions, "most benevolent. You will like him, Mr. Jones."

And I replied, "I will?"

Redleigh said, "Get along. We'll meet again. Go meet your spider roommate. Good luck."

I tipped back my glass to take a last swallow. And then I turned, eyes shut, and said to myself, Luck. My God!

I touched a button beside a door panel that slid open, and I walked along a dimly lit corridor till I came to room number 9. I touched the identity pad and the door glided open wide.

But wait, I said to myself. I can't go in. Look at my hands. Great God, they're shaking.

I stood there, unmoving. My roommate was inside, I knew. He had come from a far world and was a giant spider, or so they had said. Hell, I thought, step in.

I took three steps into the room and froze.

For in the far corner of the cubicle there was a huge shadow. Something was there, but not there.

"It can't be," I whispered to myself. "It simply can't be."

"A spider," something whispered from the far side of the room.

The large shadow trembled.

I flinched back into the doorway.

"And," the whisper continued, "a shadow of a spider? No. Stand still."

I stood still as commanded and watched as the room was illuminated and the shadow fell away and there before me was a great figure, a creature some seven feet tall and colored the most peculiar shade of green.

"Well," came the whisper again.

I replied as steadily as I could. "What can I say?"

"Anything," came the whisper.

"Once," I replied, "I went to see Michealangelo's *David.* It was tall. I circled it."

"And?"

"You look to be at least as big around as that great work."

I moved forward and began to circle the creature, which didn't move. I was, nevertheless, trembling.

The shadows continued to melt, and the shape of the creature became more apparent.

"Quell," came the whisper again. "That is my name. I have come a long way, some ten million miles and five light-years. Here on your world, judging by your size, I'd say your god has just one half-cracked eye awake.

On our world, God jumped with a shout of creation, thus our great height."

And the creature stood, even taller.

I stared at the face and said, "You—your mouth hardly moves."

The thing named Quell replied, "But my thoughts move as do yours. So," said the creature, "tell me, Jack, would you slay the giant?"

"I—" I stammered.

"I read the beanstalk in your mind."

"Damn!" I cried. "Forgive me," I said. "This is my first meeting with a telepath."

"Let me save you from damnation," said my roommate. "Once more, my name is Quell. And yours?"

"You know my name," I said. "You read minds."

"But out of politeness," Quell replied, "I pretend otherwise."

The great creature reached down with one of his appendages. I put forward my hand, and we touched.

"Ishmael Hunnicut Jones," I said.

"Well," said Quell. "That name has traveled out of your Bible and into this age of space."

"Which is much the way you've come," I said.

"Five light-years off," said Quell. "I was in deep freeze for five whole years, as cold as death. I slept the time away. It is good to be awake again. Am I not strange?"

"Oh, no," I said.

"Oh, yes," said Quell, with something like a laugh. "If thoughts fly, I catch them. That must be strange to you. And you must also be thinking that I have too many eyes, too many ears, far too many fingers, greenish skin—certainly strange. And yet I look at you and see that you have only two eyes, two tiny ears, five little fingers on each of only two hands. So then we are both—look at us—quite amusing. And both, finally . . . human."

"Yes," I said, seeing the truth in this. "Oh yes, that is human."

Quell was provoked to some sort of humor, for he went on and said, "So now, Ishmael, shall I grind your bone to make my bread, or shall we be friends?"

I flinched, prepared to back off, but I caught myself and laughed instead, and said, "Friends, yes friends, I think."

And Quell repeated, "Friends."

Later we left our cubicle and went exploring, down into the lower levels of the immense academy.

We walked among the philosophical robots who sat silhouetted among firefly lights to speak in tongues from ancient times.

"Plato," I said. "Aristotle," I went on. "Behold us. What do you see?"

And the Plato robot said, “Two terrible and fine, ugly and beautiful children of nature.”

And Quell asked, “Ah, but what is *nature*?”

Socrates answered, sparks showering, “God surprising himself with odd miracles of flesh.”

And Aristotle, a strange little plastic robot, continued: “And theirs is nothing odder or miraculous, then.”

Quell reached out and touched my forehead with one of his long, finely tufted finger-legs and said, “Ishmael.”

I responded warmly, and touched the downy chest of my new friend. “Quell, from the far islands of the great Andromeda Nebula. Quell.”

“We shall study together,” said Quell.

“Listen together, learn together, explore together,” I added.

And we did indeed listen to the voice of our robot philosopher teachers, who continued to speak in tongues various and strange during the next days, weeks, and months of our training. No one told us where we’d be going, what would be asked of us, or how long we would remain Earth-bound in these vast caverns of learning.

But finally the day came that the robot instructors’ talk, their babble, their murmurs, faded. We arrived at the lecture hall one morning and everything was still.

On the video screen were our names, and the words, "Orders received. Report for duty."

Quell observed, "Our studies appear to be at an end."

"If so," I said, "our life begins. Let us find our rocket."

We returned to our room, where our orders were awaiting us. We collected our gear and, donning our jet-packs, rose into the air and flew. The clouds gave way, the birds parted, and at last we landed at the great launching area of Cape Kennedy. We were surrounded by skyscraper gantries, gleaming rockets, the persistent buzz of intense activity.

I stared around me, stunned by the immense size of it all.

"Look, Quell, there, and there! Rockets! At least two dozen. Listen to the names: *Apollo 149, Mercury 77, Jupiter 215.* And there . . ."

Quell finished for me. "The *Cetus 7.*"

I stared at the gleaming cylinder, towering above all the other craft. "The largest interstellar ship ever built," I said, in awe.

Quell mused, "I wonder if, in their dreams, your Bach and Beethoven ever built such as these?"

A voice broke our reverie. "They did, oh yes they did."

We turned to find an old man in a faded astronaut's suit emerging from the shadow of a gangway. He spoke, saying simply, "Hello, friends."

Quell must have scanned the stranger's mind, for he replied, "We are no friends of yours."

The old man chuckled mirthlessly and continued. "You're quick to judge me, telepath. Be quicker still. Is the *Cetus 7* to be your ship?"

"It is," I replied.

The old man groaned. "Ah, you tread the rim of the Abyss. Pull back, if you know what's good for you."

Quell uttered a curse from his far world and pulled at my elbow. "Let's go, Ishmael. No need to listen to this one's false warnings."

The old man pursued us. "You, young man, do you know that spaceship's captain?"

"Not eye to eye," I said, turning back, curious.

"Eye to eye! My God, you've touched the nerve. For when you meet him, do not look into his eyes. Be warned—he has none."

"None?" I asked. "Blind?"

"No, stricken's more the word. Burnt blind in space some years ago. Ah, but *you* knew it," the old man said, turning to Quell.

"No, I did not," said Quell, tugging at my arm again. "And we'll hear no more from you."

But the old man would not be silenced. "You've already heard it, my friend, for you have just read the whole inside of my mind. You've seen. Now tell your young friend what you've learned. Tell him what's in store."

I shook off Quell's hand and stood waiting.

The old astronaut came closer and spoke very clearly. "What burnt the captain blind? Where? When? How? You may well ask. Was he a priest of space, chasing God, and God spun and struck darkness at him in one blow? Is your captain all in one smooth piece, or do the ragged edges show where he was sewn back up? Does midnight still peek out through those raw holes the doctors could not mend? Was he born an albino, or did terror bleach him like a terrible snow?"

I turned to look at Quell to see how he was taking all this, and the immense shadow that was Quell trembled in the sunlight but would not give answer.

The old astronaut, triumphant, moved yet closer.

"Now hear this. Aboard that ship, far out in space, there'll come a time when you see land—a world on the horizon—where there is no land, find time where there is no time; when ancient kings will reflesh their bones and reseat their crowns. Then, oh then, ship, ship's captain, ship's men, all, all will be destroyed! All save one."

My hands were fists. I stepped toward the old man in anger, but he backed off to finish.

"Believe me. The *Cetus 7* is no fair ship. It is its captain's. And the captain is forever lost." And finally he turned and started to walk away.

"Wait," I cried. "Hold on. What is your name?"

The old man paused, as if searching for an answer.

"Elijah. Name's Elijah. Good morning to you, friends, morning."

He spread his arms and, a moment later, where he had been was darkness.

Quell and I stood, abandoned, as a swift shadow passed over us, and the voice came one more time from above, fading, "Morning, morning."

Before either of us could say a word, there came an immense sound of thunder as a rocket, perhaps five miles distant, took off shuddering, filling the sky with color; the crimson and white flashes of ascension. As the sound receded, we became aware of sudden activity around us—the stirrings of technicians and robots and astronauts, the sounds of radios and electronic pulses, the shadows of rockets connecting to gantries, ready to lift into the universe.

Quell at last said, "It's time to go. Our ship is waiting. Ishmael, attend, we must aboard."

And so we continued on to the *Cetus 7*.

Chapter 2

Oh, the logistics of the rocket. Computerize the billion and one decisions. Ten thousand nursing bottles filled with super-homogenized gunk for space children. Fresh air produced by glass-enclosed botanical gardens. Sweat recycled into sweet water by machines.

Ring all the bells and klaxons. Flash the lights and prepare the thunders. Men and women run.

Quell and I stood by the gantry, staring up at the giant ship. It had been a week since our strange encounter with Elijah, seven days filled with intense activity as the *Cetus 7* crew, of which we were now members, prepared the ship for voyage.

"Quell," I said, "at no time in the last week, in all the rush and work, upon or around the ship, have we seen—blind or otherwise—the prophesied captain of our ship."

Quell shut his yes and cocked his strange head.

"Him," he whispered.

"What?" I urged. "What?"

Quell murmured, "He is near." And he turned and pointed up at the gantry. Its elevator was slowly rising and within the cage we saw a lone, dark figure.

"There is our captain," said Quell.

The spaceman's chapel. I had come to say a prayer before liftoff the next morning. Quell accompanied me, although I knew not to what god he prayed, if any. The muted light soothed our eyes after the blinding glare of the launching pad. Within the quiet and sacred space we stared up at the curved panoramic ceiling and there we saw, floating, the translucent shapes of men and women long lost in space. Soft murmurs emanated from them, a multitudinous whispering.

"And those? Why?" said Quell.

I watched the floating shapes and said, "Memorials, images, and voices of those who have died and are buried forever in space. Here, in the high air of the cathedral, at dawn and at dusk, their souls are projected, their voices broadcast, in remembrance."

Quell and I stood and listened and watched.

One lost voice recited, "David Smith, lost near Mars, July 2050."

Another, higher, softer, said, "Elizabeth Ball, adrift beyond Jupiter, 2087."

And a third, sonorous, again and again, "Robert Hinkston, killed by meteor swarm, 2063, buried in space."

Another whisper: "Buried."

A further sound: "Lost."

And all the whispers at once, repeating: "In space, in space, in space."

I took Quell's arm and turned him toward the front of the chapel. "There," I said, pointing. "In the pulpit, at any moment, we will see a man who died nearly a hundred years ago, but so remarkable a man was he that they computerized his soul, tracked his voice, made circuitries of his merest breath."

At that, the lights rose to illuminate a figure that was rising behind the pulpit.

"Father Ellery Colworth," I murmured.

"A robot?" said Quell, quietly.

"Yes," I said, "but more. Before us is the gentle *essence* of the man."

The lights dimmed somewhat as the incredible three-dimensional duplicate of Father Ellery Colworth began to speak.

"Is God dead?" he said. "An old question now. But once, hearing it, I laughed and replied: Not dead, but simply sleeping until you chattering bores shut up!"

There was a soft sound of laughter all around Quell and me, which faded as Father Colworth continued.

"A better answer is yet another question: Are *you* dead? Does the blood move in your hand, does that hand move to touch metal, does that metal move to touch Space? Do wild thoughts of travel and migration stir your soul? They do. Thus you live. Therefore God lives. You are the thin skin of life upon an unsensing Earth, you are that growing edge of God which manifests itself in hunger for Space. So much of God lies vibrantly asleep. The very stuffs of worlds and galaxies, they know *not* themselves. But here, God stirs in his sleep. You are the stirring. He wakes, you are that wakening. God reaches for the stars. You are His hand. Creation manifest, you go in search. He goes to find, you go to find. Everything you touch along the way, therefore, will be holy. On far worlds you will meet your own flesh, terrifying and strange, but still your own. Treat it well. Beneath the shape, you share the Godhead.

"You Jonahs traveling in the belly of a new-made metal whale, you swimmers in the far seas of deep space, blaspheme not against yourselves or the frightening twins of yourselves you find among the stars, but ask to understand the miracles which are Space, Time, and Life in the high attics and lost birthing-places of Eternity. Woe to you if you do not find all life most holy, and coming to lay yourself down cannot say, O Father God, you waken me. I waken Thee. Immortal, together we then walk upon the waters of deep space in the new morn which names itself: Forever."

The congregation—above and below—softly repeated the word, "Forever, forever."

There was a swell of soft music from somewhere in the heavens as Father Ellery Colworth finished, his figure went dark, and his silhouette was seen descending silently behind the podium.

In the long silence that came upon us I wept.

I lay awake that night in my berth aboard the *Cetus 7.*

Quell was already asleep. Rain patterns, simulated to aid slumber, fell on our faces and behind us on the wall.

The voice of a clock repeated, very softly, "Tick tock, two o'clock . . . tick tock, two o'clock."

At last I spoke.

"Quell, awake?"

And his mind spoke to me silently from across the room.

"Part of my mind, yes, the rest sleeps. I dream of the old man who warned us."

"Elijah? Did you believe him, that our captain is blind?"

"Yes. That much is common knowledge."

"And that he is mad?"

"That we must discover for ourselves."

"But by that time, mightn't it be too late, Quell?"

The soothing rain patterns continued to fall on my cheeks and the walls. There was a faint rumble of thunder from beyond.

"Quell? What, is all of you asleep now? Good companion, lie there. Your body the strange color of a world I will never see. Cold blood but warm heart; your mouth silent but your mind, even in sleep, breathing friendship."

Quell's voice, within my head, murmured drowsily, "Ishmael."

"Quell, thank God for you in the days ahead."

From all around me Quell's voice repeated, "Ishmael . . . Ishmael."

Chapter 3

A voice boomed over the loudspeakers. "The captain is in quarters, prepare for countdown."

The crew all hurried to their assigned stations, suited up and strapped in. The great doors were shut and sealed, the gantries rolled away, the engines fired up.

"Minus one and counting."

We lay waiting for the fire-wind to seize and throw us at the sky.

And seize and throw it did.

Oh my God, I thought. Help me to shout, "We rise, we rise."

But silence took us, like penitent monks, to its bosom.

For even the thundering rocket, which rips the soul on Earth, walks silently some few miles high, treads the stars without footfall, as if in awe of the great cathedral of space.

Free, I thought. No gravity. No gravity! Free. Oh, Quell, I find it most pleasant to be . . . alive.

Safely in orbit, let out of our constraints, I asked, "And now, what do we do?"

"Why, collect data," said one of the crew.

"Add and subtract constellations," said another.

"Photograph comets," said a third. "Which means, capture God's skeleton in an X-ray."

Another crew member said, "I grabbed a flash of those passing comets. From such huge ghosts of suns, I borrow cups of energy to power our ship. Sweet alchemy, my game, but fine fun pumps my blood. All round lies death, but I greet even Death with, look, this grin."

It was First Mate John Redleigh. I touched a computer screen, which whispered his name, and I saw there his log of the first hours of our journey: *August 22, 2099. Out of sight of land, yes, out of sight of the blessed land, which means all Earth and those we hold dear upon it. All faces, names, souls, remembrances, streets, houses, towns, meadows, seas—gone. All longitudes, latitudes, meridians, hours, nights, days, all time, yes, time, too, gone. Christ, guard my soul. How lonely.*

And to me Quell set free his thoughts: "Friend, I read minds, not futures. Space is large. They say it curves. Perhaps our end is our beginning. Our destination: far, very far, three mystery comets to be found by us in one constellation. Chart their course and map their routes, take their temperatures."

"How long will we travel?" I asked.

"Ten years," came the answer.

"My God, how boring," I said.

"No," said Quell, "for see how your God sends His meteors to entertain us."

"Meteor strike!" a voice cried. "Deck seven. All hands report!"

We ran. All ran to the sounds of bells and klaxons and worked to repair the ship's hull.

And at last I stood, back inside the hatch, taking off my helmet along with the rest of the crew.

And so it went, day in, day out—our ship hurtling through space, each of us with his assigned task, measuring, scanning, calculating, plotting a safe course among the broken stars.

And yet, with all this happening, still, after forty days out in space, not once did we see our captain. He stayed locked up in his cabin. But sometimes, at three or so in the deep morning, I heard the hiss of the elevator shaft, like a long, drawn-out sigh, and knew he was passing, rising up from the interior living and work levels to the outermost deck of his great ship, restricted to all but our ghost leader.

We all listened and heard.

In private, Downs said, "What does he do, up there? I hear he suits up, goes out alone, tethered by just one line."

Someone answered, "Fool, he plays games with meteors, reaching out as if to catch them, even though he cannot possibly see them coming."

And Quell added, "He shows no trust in our radar screens. Blind, he thinks he sees clearer and beyond the human eye."

"Sees what?" I asked. "Quell, you catch his thoughts. What?"

Quell was silent for a few moments, then said, "My mind hears, but the captain's mouth must speak. It is not for me to say. When he finds what he searches for, he will let us know. He—"

Suddenly Quell put his strange hands to his face, and from far off we heard the captain's cry over the intercom.

"No, no!" Quell yelled, and fell to his knees. He collapsed before us, and contorted one of his hands into a fist, eyes shut.

Quell shook his fists at the unseen stars. "Gah!" cried Quell, as if possessed. "No more of this, no more!"

And, suddenly, all was quiet. No sound came from the intercom, and Quell's arm dropped to the deck. He stood, weakened, shaken by this strange thing that had happened.

I went to my friend. "Quell," I said. "Tell me what just happened. That was not you, was it? That was the captain. You knew the captain's mind, you acted as he did, yes?"

"No," said Quell, quietly.

"Yes," I insisted. "You have no reason to defy the stars. It was he who raised his fist at the universe."

But Quell refused to respond, turning his gaze upward instead.

From First Mate John Redleigh's log: *Fifty days out. Correction: twelve hundred hours out from Earth. Student, do your sums. Computer, electro-psychoanalyze my soul. Thrust your finger, First Mate Redleigh, in a computer socket. What would you find? John Redleigh, born 2050, Reedwater, Wisconsin. Father, a maker of outboard motors. Mother, a baker of children, a dozen in all, of which the plainest of plain bread is old John Redleigh. Old, I say. Old when I was ten, long gone in senility by thirteen. Married a fine plain woman at twenty-two; filled the nursery by twenty-five. Read occasional books, thought occasional thoughts. Ah, God, Redleigh, haven't you more to put in this damn* *machine? Are you so stale, flat, unbumped, untouched, unscarred, unmoved? Have you no nightmare dreams, secret murders, drugs, or drink in your soul? Is your heart missing, the pulse spent? Did you give over when you were thirty, or were you ever more than a dry biscuit, an unbuttered bun, flat wine? Pleasantly sensual, but never passionate. A good husband, fair friend, far traveler, without worry, coming and going so quietly that God himself never noticed. And when you die, Redleigh, will even one horn sound? Will one hand flutter, one soul cry, one tear drop, one door slam? What's your sum? Let's finish it. There, there it is: zero. Did my secret self put those ciphers there? Feed zero, get zero? So I, John Redleigh, sum myself.*

"You there," said Redleigh, as I passed him outside the door to the captain's cabin.

"Sir," I said.

"Don't jump. What are you doing here? Shouldn't you be on the quarterdeck?"

"Well, sir," I said, nodding at the captain's door. "Six days. Isn't that a long time for the captain to be shut in? I can't help but wonder . . . Is he all right? I have an urge to knock upon his door."

Redleigh regarded me for a moment, then said, "Well, then . . ."

I stepped quietly to the door and rapped upon it lightly.

"No, no," said Redleigh. "Let me show you."

And he stepped up and knocked hard on the door with his fist.

He waited a moment, then knocked again.

I said, "Does he never answer, then?"

"If he knew that God Himself were out here, he might venture forth for a chat. But you or me? No."

Suddenly there was the sound of a bell, a klaxon, and from the intercom a voice spoke: "Hear this! Captain's inspection. All hands assemble, main deck. All hands, Captain's inspection."

And we turned and ran.

All gathered, five hundred strong, on the main deck.

"In line!" called Redleigh, from the head of the assembly. "He's coming, the captain is coming. Tenshun!"

There was a faint hum, a touch of electrical sound, which wavered like a swarm of insects.

The door to the main deck hissed open, and the captain was there. He stepped forward three steady, slow paces and stopped.

He was tall, well proportioned, and his uniform was completely white. The great shock of his hair was almost white, with faint traces of gray.

Over his eyes he wore a set of opaque radar-vision glasses, in which danced small firefly electric traces.

To a man, we held our breath.

At last he spoke.

"At ease."

And, as one, we let out our breath.

"Redleigh," the captain said.

"All present, sir."

The captain traced the air with his hands. "Yes, the temperature has gone up ten degrees. All present, indeed."

He moved along the front line, then stopped, one hand out, hovering near my face.

"Ah, here's one who runs the very furnace of youth. Your name?"

"Sir," I said. "Ishmael Hunnicut Jones."

"God, Redleigh," said the captain, "isn't that the sound of Blue Ridge wilderness or the scarred red hills of Jerusalem?"

Without waiting for a response, he continued, "Well, now, Ishmael. What do you see that I don't?"

Staring at him, I pulled back, and from the far side of my mind, in a panic, I whispered, "Quell?"

Suddenly I knew that if I should seize the captain's dark machine electric lenses, behind them I would find eyes the color of minted silver, of fish that had never been born. White. Oh, God, this man is white, all white.

And in my head I heard Quell, a shadow upon the air: "Some years ago the universe set off a light-year immensity of photographic flash. God blinked and bleached the captain to this color of sleeplessness and terror."

"What?" the captain demanded, for he had sensed our thoughts.

"Nothing, sir," I lied. "And there is nothing I can see that you do not."

I waited for his reply, but none was forthcoming. Instead, he turned and walked back to the head of the assembly and spoke. "How runs a ship in space, men?"

The crew murmured, and one replied, "With tight seams and oxygen suits at the ready, sir."

"Well said," the captain replied, and continued. "And how do you treat a meteor, men?"

This time I gave him the answer. "A seven-second patch and all hands saved, sir."

The captain paused at this, and then gravely asked, "Then how do you swallow a flaming comet whole, men?"

Silence.

"No answer?" thundered the captain.

Quell wrote invisibly on the air. "They have not as yet seen such comets, sir."

"They have not," the captain said. "And yet such comets do come by. Redleigh?"

Redleigh touched a control pad and a star chart descended from the ceiling before us. It was a three-dimensional work of art, a chart-maker's multi-textual dream of the universe.

The captain reached out a blind hand.

"So, here, in miniature, is the universe."

The star chart blinked.

The captain went on. "Will your eyes accomplish what mine, gone dead, cannot? From the regions of the Horsehead Nebula, among a billion fires, one special light burns. Blind, I feel its presence thus."

He touched the center of the screen. At that instant, a vast, long, beautiful comet was illumined before us.

"Do I touch the maelstrom, Redleigh?" the captain said.

"Yes, sir," replied Redleigh, as the crew whispered at the vast beauty revealed.

"Closer. Brighter," commanded the captain.

The image of the comet brightened to an immense ghost.

"So," said the captain. "Not a sun, a moon, or a world. Who'll name it?"

"Sir," said Redleigh, gently. "That is merely a comet."

"No!" shouted the captain. "It is not *merely* a comet. *That* is a pale bride with flowing veil come back to bed her lost unbedded groom. Isn't she lovely, men? A holy terror to the sight."

We stood silent, waiting.

Redleigh, moving closer, said, "Captain, is that not the comet that first passed Earth some thirty years ago?"

And I, half-remembering, spoke and gave its name: "Leviathan."

"Yes!" the captain said. "Speak up! Again!"

"Leviathan," I repeated, wondering what was going on. "The largest comet in history."

The captain whirled away from the star screen and turned his blind gaze upon us. "The brute chemistry of the universe thrown forth in light and trailing nightmare. Leviathan!"

"Was it not Leviathan, Captain," said Redleigh, softly, "that put out your eyes?"

The men murmured and stared harder at the beautiful beast.

"But to give me great vision!" the captain said. "Yes! Leviathan! I saw it close. I touched the hem of its great million-mile-long bridal veil. And then that virgin whiteness, jealous of my loving glance, rubbed out my sight. Thirty, thirty, thirty years ago. I still see it on my inner lids every night, so passing strange, so full of Arctic miracles, that huge white thunderhead of God. I ran to it. I offered up my fevered soul. And it *snuffed me out*! And then it ran, leaving me. Yet look."

He touched the three-dimensional chart and the comet brightened yet again, loomed even larger.

"Leviathan returns," said the captain. "I have waited thirty long years, and the moment has finally come. And I have chosen you, men, to be with me on this starship to rush and meet that downfell light, which having once doomed me now cycles round to doom itself. Soon, I will lift my hands—*your* hands—to make that strike."

The men stirred, but said nothing.

"What?" the captain said. "Silence?"

"Sir," Redleigh said, "that is not our mission, our destination. What of our loved ones on Earth . . ."

"They will know of it! And they will celebrate when we have bled this beast and interred it in the Coalsack Nebula burial ground."

"But questions will be asked, sir," said Redleigh.

"And we will answer those questions. And we will complete our mission. *After* we have dealt with Leviathan. We must learn the stuffs of pure destruction. Look on Leviathan! What is it? Some dread thing torn from out God's throat when He knew darkness in His sleep?

Gone evil with time, gone tired with creation, did God frighten up his bones and mind and lungs in one titanic seizure to cough forth this sickening? Who knows, can guess, or tell? All I know is that old curse and bled-forth wound now terrorizes space and ravens at our heels.

"Let us speak gently now. Wherever God now is, why, spring and sweet winds play. But with Leviathan, all dies and bleeds away. Great God, I worship thee. But thy old ailment comes to winnow me and split my bones and kindle up dead eyes to half an obscene light. So madness gives me strength for this last night. Insanity makes grasp both long and broad. Once clutched and killed, Leviathan, I will turn back to my God."

We stood, as if spellbound.

Redleigh at last dared to propose: "This hell you speak of . . . is it quite that Hell?"

"Why," said the captain, "there's Death himself come round to even up old scores. God sums Himself on Earth four billion strong. But here's the beast to make that right go wrong. Within a month, this light-year creature, mid-Pacific, will submerge and murder all that's living on Earth."

"But our scientists, sir—" began Redleigh.

"Are blind!" yelled the captain. "No, worse! For even blind, I see! On other journeys, Leviathan missed our Earth by a million miles or more."

"And *this* time round," insisted Redleigh, "the calculations show that it will miss Earth by *six times* as much."

"Your wise men say Survival? I say Death," the captain roared. "Our funeral comes this way. Changed, pulled, put on new tracks by far dark worlds beyond our sight, put off by gravities of malice, Leviathan now veers to doom us. Does *no one* see or care?"

We in our ranks shifted uneasily. What our captain spoke seemed madness, and yet he was so sure, so strong.

"We must take care now," said Redleigh finally, "if what you say is true."

"Aye to that!" we yelled as one.

"Proof, now, Redleigh," said the captain. "Here are my charts." He pulled a slim disk from his coat and held it out in the direction of Redleigh's voice. "Computerize these as far as you or God can count and then beyond."

"I will take your charts, sir," said Redleigh, gravely.

"Quickly," said the captain. "Scan, study, *see*."

Redleigh turned the disk over in his hands.

"For there you will find Doom," the captain went on. "But, if serenity, sweet peace, and mild excursions are your findings, man . . . if you discover instead fair

Heaven and find green Eden, say your say with graceful data! Play the computer. If your final tune is joy, I will accept it, and turn us back toward stallion and mare meadows and fine frolics; no remorse."

"Fair put, sir."

"Where's your hand?" said the captain, reaching out upon the air.

"Here, sir."

The captain seized it. "Now man, attend. Here's one who gives his palm on palm to me. May I beg hearts and souls from all the rest?"

"They're here!" came all our voices.

"And all about!" I added.

"Aye and aye!" cried many voices.

The captain still held tight to Redleigh's hand, binding him to his compact as he cried out a final oath: "Christ's wounds swallow comets! Much thanks for that sweet sound. Men! Ours is a holy mission. There will be none greater in the history of humanity, though our sands run forever through a glass as big as Creation's landfall in far Centauri! We will save our Earth! Technicians, stand alert! Oh, men, Leviathan is a long white unhealed wound in space, a light that puts out light. Let us heal it forever. Ready the alarms. The first man who spots it gets double his pay for the journey! Squads, disperse. Fall out!"

The crew ran to their stations, all but Quell. Sensing that my friend was not with me, I pulled up short, and turned to see Quell, gazing at the captain with a look of terrible revelation. Redleigh, too, took note of Quell's expression, and stood quietly beside the captain.

The captain, feeling the silence, said, "Dismissed, Redleigh."

"Sir."

And Redleigh turned and walked away.

"Ishmael?" the captain said suddenly. "Dismissed."

"Sir!" I saluted to those blind eyes, and started to leave but hesitated to look back at the captain and Quell.

The captain sensed Quell drawing near. And yet Quell would not look at him. The captain raised a hand to touch the air near Quell's strange green face. He seized his hand back as if it was half-burnt. Then he turned and stepped back through the door leading off the main deck and the door whispered shut.

There was a long moment in which Quell's face gathered shadows of his own future. I could not bear to witness it.

And then I heard the voices of the crew, coming from all around, one by one.

"The comet Franciscus 12."

"Halley's comet."

"The comet of Pope Innocent the Third."

"The Great India comet of '88."

"The comet of Alcibiades."

And on the great star screen, one by one, I saw gigantic manifestations of comets, meteors, star clusters, all of which hung themselves on the dark.

"What *is* a comet, anyway?" I heard myself say. "Who knows, really," I answered myself. "Universal vapors. The mighty indigestion of our creator. Quell?"

Quell's thoughts touched mine.

"On my world, such comets are known as pilgrim visitors, far-traveling specters, haunters of the feast. You see? Our history has as much romantic nonsense as yours."

"Well, then," I said, "the captain has his reasons for seeking his comet, and we have ours. There's nothing like a riddle."

"A riddle," said Quell. "Let us sleep on that tonight. Perhaps in sleep, we'll dream, and in the dream, find an answer. A riddle. A riddle."

And it was in the midst of the night, while I slept, that I heard something stirring. Quell. I felt his mind move in mine and then, at last, his voice: "May all the men rise up and listen."

Then, not only in my mind, but with his tongue, Quell said the syllables that made "Elijah."

"Quell," I whispered faintly.

And then how strange it was, for it was not Quell's voice that I heard now, in the middle of the night, but the voice that spoke in his mind. It was the voice of Elijah, recalled.

"Oh, listen, hear!" said the voice that I'd last heard in the cathedral on Earth. "Aboard this ship, far out in space, there will come a time when you see land where there is no land, find time where there is no time, when ancient kings will reflesh their bones and reseat their crowns."

"What's that?" I heard from some other room along the corridor.

"Shut him off, shut him up," cried another.

"No, wait, wait," I whispered.

And Quell continued with the voice of Elijah: "Then, then, oh, then, ship, ship's captain, and ship's men, all, all will be destroyed. All save *one*!"

"All?" someone said.

"Save one," said another.

"All will be destroyed," said Quell, with the voice of Elijah.

And then he sank back into silence and slept.

I turned over but could not sleep, and sensed my crewmates in their cubicles, up and down the corridor, sleepless till dawn.

The voice clock in every cabin ticked and named the hours and at last, with no sunrise, in our minds we saw a ghost comet loom in spirit smoke above the captain's bunk, and the captain mourned his own death in his sleep.

From the log of First Mate John Redleigh: *Records dating 400 B.C. Rumors have it that Alexander the Great's death was predicted in the appearance of the comet Persephone. The comet Palestrina arrived in the year one; it may well have been the Star of Bethlehem. This much we know, but little more. The main material of a comet's body is methane gas and wintry snow, wintry snow.*

Unable to sleep, I arose and left my bunk, drawn to the captain's cabin. From outside that sealed door I could hear his nightmares within. "No," I heard him groan. "No, no, I say. Get off. Go!"

A figure came along the corridor: Redleigh. I pulled back into the shadows as the first mate pounded on the captain's door.

"Captain?"

The captain called out from within. "What? What?"

"You were having a nightmare, sir," said Redleigh.

The door opened and the captain stood there, his white hair wild. "God, I dreamt I fell, I fell, down in space, forever. Let me grasp my soul."

"Ship's log to be signed, sir," said Redleigh.

"At four in the false morning? Good, Redleigh, something to keep me from my nightmares. I'll come with you to sign. How go the star computers?"

"They burn, sir, from overuse."

"You jump to prove me wrong?"

"You have said you were right, sir," said Redleigh. "I would prove that."

The captain stepped out of his cabin, and I moved back further into the shadows, even though he could not see me. They started down the corridor, toward the main deck, and I followed along.

"I know you, Redleigh. You have no heart for this chase, do you?"

"If by 'chase' you mean our proper business of charting stars and exploring worlds . . ."

"No, no! Here!" the captain said as he emerged onto the vast main deck, nearly empty now, and pointed toward the star screen. The three-dimensional display hung brightly on the air.

"What do you know of the passage of dark planets and bright comets?"

"I think you must teach me, sir," said Redleigh.

"And I will," said the captain. "Here are a thousand thousand star-charts, stamped, runneled, and humped. Run your hand over this expanse. Touch the long mark of Halley's comet; feel the heat of the comet of Alliostro Minor. Here, the deep night plans for all God's circuitings and maunderings, all his long thoughts. God dreams joy: green Earths appear. God suffers torments: Leviathan issues from the vast portal of His raving eye and mouth. It rushes here! I know a way to meet it head-on, fast, six weeks before it destroys Earth. We must move fast to surprise it."

"Surprise?" Redleigh turned from the charts that hung so brightly on the air. "You cannot *surprise* a comet, sir. It neither lives nor cares."

"But *I* live, *I* care," said the captain.

Redleigh shrugged. "And shift the burdens of your knowledge to some great wandering child, some universal accident that prowls the worlds, homeless for eternity. I —"

"Go on," said the captain.

"Sir, if as the Reverend Colworth says, all space is one flesh with us, all worlds, suns, creatures extensions of one ground, one all-encompassing will, then that ghost you speak of, sir, that comet, that great terror-trailing monster, is but a true outmouthing of God Himself. Not his sickness and despair, but His bright will that lights the universal night. Would you stand against such breath?"

"If it wrenched my soul and burnt me blind, yes! Listen to the sound it makes this very hour, out beyond."

The captain reached out a hand, touching a screen. A loom of energy wove immense sounds throughout the ship.

Nodding at this, the captain continued. "There's the breath you spoke of. It is a cold thing. It is all the graveyards of history somehow put to space, and in its light-year shroud, ten billion on a billion men's lost souls yammer for release. I—we—go to rescue them!"

"That sound is but a dumb thing, sir, mere chemistry born of chaos, now pulled by this tidal star, now hauled by that. You may as well stop your own heart as try to stop that great pale beating."

"But if both stop at once?" said the captain, "will not my victory over it be as large as its victory over me? Small man, great traveling doom—both weigh the same when the scale is death."

"But in rending it," said Redleigh, in quiet desperation, "you rend your own flesh, Captain, which God has loaned you."

"This flesh offends me!" cried the captain. "If it is all one, God manifesting himself in minerals, light, motion, dark, or sensible man, if that comet is my sister-self come preening by to try my Job-like patience, was it not blasphemy it first tried on *me*? If I am God's flesh, why was *I* felled, struck blind? No, no! That thing is lost and evil. Its great face hovers in the abyss. Behind its mindless glare I sense the blood that oils the cogs of nightmare and the pit. And whether I perceive all this in hellfire man, sweet blood-mouthed cannibal shark, or huge white blinding mask flung down among the stars to frighten men and push them to impulse much less than human, more than bones and soul can bear, I must attack. Talk not of blasphemy to me, sir. It tried *me* at breakfast. I will dine on it *tonight*."

"Oh God," whispered Redleigh. "Oh God help us, then."

"He *does*," the captain responded. "If we are His stuffs, alive, then we sinew His arm, thrust out to stop that light-year beast. Would you turn away from this greatest hunt?"

"I would," murmured Redleigh, "and go to check my computers, sir."

Redleigh turned to leave, but stopped when the captain said, "Why then you're as mad as me. No, madder. For I distrust 'reality' and its moron mother, the universe, while you fasten your innocence to fallible devices which pretend at happy endings. Lie down with machines, rise up *castrato.* Sweet Jesus, you'll make the pope's choir yet. Such innocence quakes my bones."

"Sir," Redleigh responded. "I am against you. But don't fear me. Let the captain beware the captain. Beware of yourself . . . sir."

And once more Redleigh turned, and this time he walked away.

Chapter 4

I backed off and returned to my cabin, deeply distressed. I barely slept the hours remaining till dawn, instead tossing and turning in my bunk, while Quell lay undisturbed, dreaming who knows what alien dreams.

At the first bell, I rose and made my way to the communications deck. There I found crewman Small, bent over his console.

"Do you know that a rocket feeds itself in space?" he asked.

"Feeds? What do you mean?"

"It wallows," he explained, "like a great fish in currents of solar vibration, cosmic rays, interstellar X-ray radiations. Ever hungry, we—this ship—search for banquets of shout and shriek and echo. I sit here, day in and day out, tuned to the great onrushings of space all around us. Most of the time, all I hear is variations of anonymous sound—hum and static and vibration. And once in a while, by accident . . . listen!"

He touched a contact and from the console speaker came voices—distinct human voices. He turned his face to mine, a strange light shining there.

As we stood, we heard broadcasts that had been made to crowds on Earth, to the listening ears of people two hundred years ago. Churchill spoke and Hitler shouted and Roosevelt answered and mobs roared; there were football and baseball games from long-ago afternoons. They rose and fell, moved in and out, like ocean waves of sound.

Small said, "No sound, once made, is ever truly lost. In electric clouds, all are safely trapped, and with a touch, if we find them, we can recapture those echoes of sad, forgotten wars, long summers, and sweet autumns."

"Mr. Small," I said. "We must trap these broadcasts so we can hear them again and again. Is there more? What have you found?"

"We have come upon a fountain of Earth's younger days. Voices from centuries past. Strange radio people, ghosts of laughter, political charades. Listen."

Small fiddled with the console dial again. We heard the moment the *Hindenburg* went up in flames.

Lindbergh landed in Paris in 1927. Someone named Dempsey fought someone named Tunney in 1925. Crowds screamed in horror, mobs cheered. And then, it began to fade away.

"We're beyond them now," said Small.

"Go back!" I cried. "That is our history."

Another voice sounded from the console: "This afternoon at Number Ten Downing Street, Prime Minister Churchill . . ."

The captain strode onto the deck.

"Sir," said Small. "We have found a fountain of Earth's younger days. Voices from centuries past. Strange radio people, ghosts of laughter, political charades. Listen!"

The captain said, most sadly, "Yes, yes." And then, suddenly, "Small, Jones, leave that now. They speak but to themselves. We cannot play, nor laugh, nor weep with them. They are *dead.* And we have an appointment with the *real.*"

Small reached again for the console dial, as a final voice announced: "Line drive! Mantle safe at first!"

Then, silence.

I touched my cheek to wipe away a tear. Why do I weep? I wondered. Those voices were not my people, my times, my ghosts. And yet once they lived. Their dust stirred in my ears, and I could not stop my eyes.

Suddenly, over the ship's intercom, a voice boomed: "Blue alert. All scanning stations. Visual sighting. Star sector CV7. Visual sighting. Blue alert!"

Quell and I stood before his viewing screen, stunned at what we saw there.

"Great God," I said. "What's that?"

"A moon," said Quell.

"Yes," I said. "But what a moon. It looks so old. Much older than our own, covered with towns, cities, ancient gardens. How long do you think that moon has been spinning in space alone?"

Quell consulted his instrument panel, and zoomed in the picture.

"Ten thousand times a million years," said Quell. "Oh lovely, lovely . . . the spires, the jeweled windows, the lonely and deserted courtyards filled with dust."

And then we heard Redleigh's voice: "Stand by! Diminish speed."

And then the captain's voice cut in: "Mr. Redleigh!"

"Sir, this moon! It's very old and fine. Our mission is to explore, to find, to report."

"Yes, Redleigh, I can hear it in your voice. It is a lovely lost and wandering world, an ancient beauty, passing strange, but pass it we must. Resume course."

And over the intercom came the order: "Resume full speed. Blue alert canceled."

The image of the lost moon, which had been projected on all the screens throughout the ship, began to pass away.

"Lost again," said Quell.

And once again, the ship was surrounded by black space.

Chapter 5

From Small's console came dim voices, cloaked in static, from untold miles away: "*Lightfall 1* calling *Cetus 7. Light-fall* here. Inbound from twelve years out. *Cetus 7,* do you read?"

My God, I thought, another spacecraft.

Quell's voice touched my thoughts. "Impossible. In all these billions of miles of space. What are the chances of meeting—"

"Another spaceship?" I asked aloud.

"This is *Lightfall 1,*" came the voice again. "Shall we hang fire, *Cetus 7*?"

Men were running to the main deck from every direction, crowding around monitors.

"*Cetus 7,* request permission to approach, link, and board."

"Yes!" cried the crew.

"No!" thundered the captain.

"*Cetus 7,* please respond."

The captain instructed Small to open a communications channel to the other ship. "*Lightfall 1,* this is *Cetus 7.* Permission denied."

"*Cetus 7*—please confirm: permission denied? Do I read you?"

"You do," our captain replied.

"But my men, Captain, listen to them!"

And over the open communications channel we hear a grand clamor from the other ship, a few thousand miles off.

"Damned fools at nursery games," said our captain. "There is no time. No time!"

"Time?!" said the voice from *Lightfall 1.* "Why, for Christ's sake, that's all there is in space! God has a plentitude of time. And I? I am full of long years wandering and news of strange stars and terrible comets."

"Comets?" our captain cried.

"The greatest comet in the universe, sir!" said the commander of *Lightfall 1.*

"Stand by, then," our captain said. "Permission to come aboard."

We watched on the viewscreens as the *Lightfall 1* approached. Both ships reached out mechanical arms and grasped each other as friends. There was a dull thunk as the linkage was complete, and within the hour the *Lightfall 1*'s captain stepped aboard the *Cetus 7* and saluted.

"Jonas Enderby here, of the *Lightfall 1*."

He stepped out of the airlock, and from behind him came a dozen or so crew members of the *Lightfall 1*—dark, light; male and female; short, tall; human and alien—glancing about them. We smiled in welcome, eager to hear their story.

Later, in the communal mess, Commander Enderby raised a glass to our captain, with whom he sat at the center table. "To your health, sir. No, *mine*. My God, it's been nine months since I've had an honest-to-God drink. I'm with child! And that child is thirst."

The *Lightfall* commander drank.

"More!" he demanded.

"More, yes," our captain said. "And then speak."

"Would you like to hear of comets?" said Enderby of the *Lightfall 1*.

"I am tuned to that," replied our captain, a bright light glinting in his eye.

We all inched a little closer, as close as protocol would allow, to listen.

"God sickened in my face," said Enderby. "I am not clean yet. For it was the greatest, longest, brightest—"

Our captain cut in. "Leviathan?!"

Enderby gasped. "You know it?"

"You tracked it then?"

"Tracked it, hell, it bled me white and cracked my bones! I only just escaped with my life."

"Ah," the captain cried. "Do you hear, Redleigh?"

Enderby continued. "I do not mean to stretch the joke. It tried me, sir. It swallowed me, my ship, and crew in one great hungry gulp. We lived *in* Leviathan!"

"In! Hear that, Redleigh? In!"

The *Lightfall 1* commander went on. "You do make it sound jolly, sir."

Our captain stood, all stony silence. "I meant no offense. Of all people, I well know . . ."

"And jolly it was!" Enderby continued. "What else can one do when stuck deep in the belly of the beast? We danced a rigadoon in Leviathan's gut!"

"And yet—you're *here*!"

"Sir, it could not stomach us! We poisoned it with laughter. All round within it we rose, we fell, we rose again, mystified by Fate, hysterical with chance. We fired our laughs like cannons at its heart!"

The captain shook. "Laughter? Dancing?" he wondered.

And Enderby of the *Lightfall 1* touched his right eye. "Yes! Though before it took us into its maw, it spoiled my sight and killed this eye. See? Pure forge-cast Irish crystal. Glass! I swear. Shall I pluck it out and play at marbles?"

"No, no. Let it be," our captain said with a sigh. "I believe you."

"I see you do," Enderby replied. "Leviathan did blind me once, but completed only half the job. It would have destroyed my other eye, if it'd had the chance. But we raised such a riot that Leviathan suffered sickness and spat us out back unto the stars!"

Our captain seized Enderby's arm. *"Where?"*

"Ten million miles beyond the outermost circumscape of Saturn's transit."

"Do you hear that, Redleigh?" our captain cried. "It is still on course!"

"Course?" The *Lightfall 1* captain laughed. "What course? Do you think it *knows* what it is doing, where it is going? How can chaos be plotted, planned, *coursed*? Where is that gin? I need another drink."

Redleigh stepped forward and doled it out.

"My charts are right and true," said the captain, grabbing Redleigh's arm and spilling gin in the process. "I will go to meet that ghost!"

"On *my* recommendation?" Enderby said, astonished. "Did I make it sound too bright? Hell." He shook his head. "Here's to caps and bells and rollicking tunes. Here's to Leviathan and you, sir. May you cap its bile as it spits you out. God will that it *may* spit you out."

"We must be away, and now," the captain said, his brow glistening with sudden sweat. "All hands, on deck!"

Enderby stood and said, "But Captain, can we not stay a bit longer? My crew would do well for some more time with new faces, new friends, news of home. We are weary, and dry as sand."

"My thirst is greater," the captain thundered. "We must be off."

Enderby drained his glass and slammed it on the table. "To hell with you, sir! Go on your fool's mission, if that is what you choose."

Enderby stood, and motioned for his crew to follow. They wound their way through the corridors to the airlock doors, donned their suits, and left.

In moments, *Lightfall 1* and all its crew were gone, lost again to soundless space.

Chapter 6

Deep in the false night, our captain walked along the sleeping quarter corridors. Quell scanned his mind and spoke his words to me in whispers: "'What, pretending at sleep? Do that, and bite your bitter tongues, which hate me for spoiled games. But if Christ Himself walked through space this night—'"

And Quell, speaking in his own voice, added: "Not Christ. But one of His lost shepherds."

The next morning, Redleigh summoned Quell and me to Small's communication console. There we met crewman Downs.

"This communication occurred last night," Redleigh said, nodding at Small, who touched a contact on his console. We listened, and heard at first the usual static and pulses of space, and at last a fine voice began to speak.

"This is starship *Rachel,*" a far voice said. "Theological starship *Rachel,* the spacecraft of Pius the Wanderer, calling *Cetus 7.* Answer, *Cetus 7.*"

And the captain, switching on, said, "*Cetus 7* here."

The mournful voice of Pius filled the air. "Have you seen a small life-rocket adrift? A space storm carried it away. Fine priests were in it, pacing that comet—"

"Leviathan?!" asked the captain.

The *Rachel*'s captain responded, "Yes! My son, my *only* son, good child of God, was on that rocket. Fearless, curious. The Great White Bride, he called it. He went to search the White Bride's wake, with two other good men. And now I search for him. Will you help?"

"I have no time, sir," said our captain.

"Time!" the *Rachel*'s captain cried. "Why, I've lost my whole *life.* You must help me."

The captain spoke again. "Away! I go to redeem your son. God help you, Captain."

The *Rachel*'s captain, voice fading, said, "God *forgive* you, master of the *Cetus 7.*"

And the recording went dead. We five looked at each other, stung by the exchange. I said, "So the *Rachel,* mourning her lost children, fell away and we move toward what, annihilation?"

My companions looked away, uneasily.

Quell spoke. "Mr. Redleigh, you sent for us?"

Distantly, an airlock door opened and somewhere, above, out of sight, we felt the captain's strange magnetic tread.

Downs looked upward and said, "Is it about him?"

"Him, and more," said Redleigh. "About clouds of old radio time that spoke in tongues, which we let pass. Fellow spacefarers travel-weary and lonely. Priest ships we refuse to rescue. Jobs left undone—"

Downs cut in. "But, sir, the captain has told us that this comet is our *job*."

"Well, then," said Redleigh, "here are the captain's charts. Leviathan will strike Earth, yes?"

"Yes," we all agreed. "Why, of course, yes."

"Here is Earth," Redleigh said, pointing at the chart. "Now, Downs, light its substance. Now, let us illuminate Leviathan, there. Move both Earth and white light on their ways, here, and see how they travel. The computer sums and keeps the score. There!"

The great star chart took fire. We saw our planet Earth. We saw the comet. Earth moved. Leviathan moved. The universe wheeled. Leviathan rushed along space and Earth spun about the sun.

"There, see," said Downs. "A collision course! The comet *will* destroy Earth! Just as the captain said."

"No, it will not," said Redleigh.

And as we watched the unfolding of the great star chart, the huge comet streaked by without striking Earth.

"See, it goes," commented Redleigh. "The comet continues on, leaving Earth untouched."

We watched the comet fade.

Redleigh switched off the chart.

Downs spoke up. "Captains don't lie."

"They don't," said Redleigh, "unless they are mad. Then lying's all the truth they know. Quell?"

We looked at Quell, who shifted uneasily.

"Quell knows," said Redleigh. "Quell, these men are drowning. Give them air."

Quell remained silent with his eyes shut and when he spoke, spoke only to himself. "O fathers of time, forgive me. Here," he gestured, pulling us close into his spider arms. "Let me gather your minds. So. And thus."

We felt our souls embraced. We looked up. Quell had gathered us and bound it to the soul and mind and voice of the captain.

From the uppermost deck of the ship, beneath the stars, we heard our captain cry, "I think I see!"

We were shaken, for we did hear him clearly, though he was impossibly far away.

Quell shook his head and pulled back and the captain's voice faded.

"Quell," I urged. "Go on! Please. We must hear."

Quell gathered us to him again. There was fire in his eyes and strange green cheeks. The captain's voice grew strong again as it moved through Quell.

"Yes, I almost think I do. Far worlds, long dead, break on these eyes with living sights, again, again, again, and say: 'We live! Remember us! Oh, think on us. Our sins forgive! Our virtues celebrate, though flesh and blood, and blood's sweet will are gone. And with it that despair called hope, which wakes us at dawn. Remember us!'

"You are remembered, though I knew you not. Your ancient plight inspires, your nightmare's not forgot . . . I keep it here kindled with my own; your ghost of outrage I give flesh and bone; your spirit war moves my arm to smite; you speak my noon and instruct my night.

"As you to me, so I to other worlds will one day be when this night's deeds, the things we say and act out on this lonely stage, one million years on from this hour will break and flower on some far shore, where such as you look up, and behold, and know our loss or gain, life's wakening or death's yawn."

And again, quietly, our captain continued.

"So we, like they, pass on, forever ghosts, knocking at portals, prying at doors, speaking our actions, re-promising old dreams, welcome or unwelcome. Yet on we go, light-year on light-year, and no one there beyond to know. Thus they and theirs, and we and ours will shadow-show eternity, two films projected to opposite screens and nothing and nothing and nothing in between.

"I murder or murdered will be this night. But there, trapped and traveled in storms of light I am not yet born.

"O God I would be that child, to start again and, starting, know some peace on a clean baptismal morn."

Quell let us go, dropping his arms, his eyes closed.

"Oh, God . . .," Redleigh said, touched and anguished.

"God, yes," said Small. "No more, no more of this. It must be stopped."

Quell drew in a breath, and then again the captain's voice came. "Eternal noons, I asked, O Lord! Eternal midnight, my reward. O whiteness there! My pale and wandering lust. O spirit dread, stand forth! This time I will not swerve. My path is fixed beyond the gravities! Tracked like the worlds that fire about the sun, so runs my soul in one trajectory.

"Blind, my body aches and is one eye! I'll weave eclipse to darken you who dared to darken me. Your veil will be your winding sheet. Your mindless gossamer I'll bind to strangle you. Leviathan! Leviathan!"

We felt his hands reach out to grasp and hold and kill.

And, last: "Can I do this and bank my fires?"

Quell echoed, in his own weary voice, "Fires."

And we were silent, standing there, and the captain said no more.

Chapter 7

At last Redleigh said, "Well?"

And Downs lifted his head and looked straight at the first mate and said, "That was unlawful, uncommon, criminal eavesdropping. We have no right!"

"Upon uncommon *dangers*!"

"Would you mutiny, sir?" said Small.

Redleigh pulled back, a horrified look on his face. "Mutiny?!"

Quell broke in. "He would . . . *take over.*"

And we answered mutely, with our own horrified faces.

Redleigh said, "Have you not just heard what is in his heart, what he intends to do?"

Downs replied, "We have. But those thoughts of the captain's which we have *borrowed* . . . why, how do they differ from ours? All men are poet-murderers in their souls, ashamed to bleed it out."

Small said, "You ask us to judge *thoughts*!"

"Judge actions then!" Redleigh responded. "Leviathan comes. We are changing our course to meet it. Someone has tampered with the computer—just twenty-four hours ago it said one thing, now it says another."

Downs said, "And so it goes with machines. Astronomical sums are nice, but blood is best. Flesh is easier. Mind and will are excellent. The captain is all these. The computer doesn't know I *live*. The captain does. He looks, he sees, he interprets, he decides. He tells me where to go. And as he is my captain, so I go."

"Straight to hell," said Redleigh.

"Then hell it is." Downs shrugged. "The comet's birthing-place. The captain has the beast in his sights. I hate beasts too. My captain rouses me with *No!* And I am his dearest echo."

Little said, "And I!"

"Quell?" said Redleigh, turning to the green alien.

"I have said too much," said Quell. "And all of it the captain's."

"Ishmael?" said Redleigh.

"I," I replied, "am afraid."

Downs and Small stepped away. "Excused, Mr. Redleigh?"

"No!" shouted Redleigh. "Sweet Jesus, he's blinded you, too. How can I make you *see*?"

"It's late in the day for that, Redleigh," said Small.

"But see you will, dammit! I'm going to the captain. Now. You must stand *behind* if not *with* me. You'll hear it from his own mouth."

"Is that a command, sir?"

"It is."

"Well, then," said Small, "aye, sir."

"And aye, I guess," said Downs.

And the three crewmen walked away, Quell and me following, listening for the strange electronic pulse of the captain, near but far.

Chapter 8

"Mr. Redleigh, you have come to mutiny."

The captain had granted us entrance to his quarters and he stood within, facing us, his strange white eyes seeming to stare.

"Sir," said Redleigh. "The simple fact is—"

The captain interrupted. "Simple? The sun's temperature is 20,000 degrees. Yet it will burn Earth. Simple? I distrust people who come with plain facts and then preach calamities. Now, Redleigh, listen. I am giving over command of this spacecraft to you."

"Captain!" cried Redleigh in surprise.

"Captain no more. You will take the credit for the grand destiny ahead."

"I have no desire for destinies," said Redleigh.

"Once you know it, you will desire it. You come with facts? Leave with *more* than that. Who has seen a comet up close?"

"Why no one, sir, save you."

"Who has touched a comet's flesh?"

"Again, no one that we know."

"What is a comet's stuff that we should run to welcome it?"

"To the point, Captain."

"The point! We go as fishers with our nets. We go as miners to a deep and splendid mine of minerals both raw and beautiful. That school of fish, which is Leviathan in space, is most certainly the largest treasure of all time. Dip our nets in that and bring up miracles of fish, pure energies that put the miracles at Galilee to shame. In that vast treasure house we shall unlock and take of as we will. There must be ten billion mines, so vast their glitter would burn your eyes. Such black diamonds fall from space each night, all night, throughout all our lives, and burn to nothing. We catch that rain. We save its most bright tears to sell in common markets most uncommonly. Who says no to this?"

"Not I—as yet," said Redleigh, warily.

"Then siphon off the very breath of that great ghost. Its breath is hydrogen and mixtures of such flaming vapors as will light entire civilizations for our children's children's lifetimes. Such energy, harnessed, controlled, collected, kept, released, will work atomic wonders for our race, and cause such further wonders of recompense. I see rare bank accounts that will retire us all early, on to madness."

"Madness?"

"The madness of pleasure and the good life and sweet ease. Leviathan's breath and body are yours to bank for cash and credit. As for myself, I ask a single thing: leave its soul to me. Well?"

"Why, if that's the sort of shower that falls from space," Downs said, "I'll run out in that rain."

"Yes! As children run in spring showers!"

And I thought, His poetry has won me, but not his facts.

The captain now turned to Quell and said, "Good Quell, you read my mind. Are not fair weather there and rain and minted silver coins lost in a high new grass?"

And Quell had no answer.

"Redleigh?"

"Damn you, sir."

"No sooner damned than saved," replied the captain. "Salvation rings me in. Listen to its sound. Small? Downs?"

"Aye, sir!" said both.

"Quell? Ishmael?" A pause. "Your silence is affirmative." And, turning to Redleigh: "Where is your mutiny now?"

"You have *bought* them, sir!" said Redleigh.

"Bid then, and buy them back," replied the captain.

Later, in the privacy of my own bunk, I made the following entry in my personal journal: *We have run from old radio voices, shunned lost moons with lost cities, refused to share glad drinks and fine laughs with lonely spacemen, and ignored rare priests searching for their lost sons. The list of our sins grows long. Oh God! I must listen then, to space, to see what else is there, what other crimes we might commit in ignorance.*

Putting the journal down, I touched a contact on the room's radio set. At first there was nothing but cold static and then came music, a symphony stranger than any I'd ever heard.

I turned it up and listened with my eyes shut.

The sound of the music caused the sleeping Quell to stir. I switched it off, and from his side of the room came Quell's voice, urgent.

"Turn it back on, quickly."

I touched the contact again, and the music returned. It was beautiful, a requiem for the living to be mourned like the dead.

I knew it haunted Quell, for his mind now embraced mine.

"Oh, listen," he whispered. "Do you hear? Music from my far world."

"Yours?" I said. "Billions of miles off? Oh, Lord!"

"Lord indeed," said Quell. "Music that has traveled all the way from my galaxy, and more. That is the music of my father's father's suffering and death."

The music continued to play, somber and funereal.

I felt tears sting my eyes for no reason, and Quell went on: "The dirge my grandfather composed for his own funeral, his great lament."

"Why, listening," I wondered aloud, "do I mourn for myself?"

Then Quell reached out with an unseen hand and an invisible mind and spoke to Downs.

"Downs," he said. "Can you put aside your ship's tasks for a while and make me a special space suit?"

"I would, sir, if I knew how," came Downs's reply.

"I will draw it," said Quell, "and give you the plan. Come here now."

"Quell!" I said, alarmed. "What's this about?"

I sat up, and saw Quell at his desk, his strange hand drawing a strange shape on the computer screen before him.

"There," said Quell. "The proper suit, decorated with symbols of my lost world."

"Is this to be your coffin, then?" said Downs, as he entered our room and looked at Quell's plans.

"All beings in space suits inhabit future coffins of their own use and shape. This is but a darker thing. Cut it from night, solder it with shadows."

"But why?" Downs wanted to know. "Why do you want a suit of death?"

"Listen," I urged.

I turned up the otherworldly music. Downs listened and his eyes trembled and his hands began to move.

"God, look at my fingers. It's as if they have a mind of their own. That dirge does this. Oh, Quell, good Quell, I guess there's no way but that I must make this terrible suit."

"Quell," I interrupted, "that music has been to the far side of the universe and back. Why does it arrive here, *now*?"

"Because it is the proper time."

"Quell!"

But silent, he sat there, staring in a fixed position at nothingness.

"Quell," I urged. "Listen to me."

Downs put a hand on my shoulder. "He doesn't hear you."

"He must feel what I think!" I replied.

"No," said Downs. "I've seen the like before. Whether among the natives in the lost seas of Earth or the far side of space, it's much the same. *Death* is speaking to him."

"Don't listen, Quell!" I said, and put my hands over his ears, which was stupid, for as Downs then said: "His whole body hears. How will you stop that?"

"Like this!" I cried. "Like *this*!"

I wrapped my arms around Quell and held him tight, very tight.

Downs said, softly, "Let it be. You might as well try to breathe life into the white marble on a tomb."

"I will!" I said. "Oh, Quell, it's Ishmael here! Your friend. Dammit, Quell, I ask, no, I *demand*—let it go! This very instant, stop! I'll be very angry with you, if this goes on. I won't speak to you again! I'll, I'll . . ." And here I paused, for I could not breathe. "I shall weep."

I was surprised by my own tears and pulled back to see them falling on my numbed palms. I held out my hands to Quell, showing him those tears.

"Quell, look, please look," I pleaded.

But Quell did not see.

I tried to think what I must do.

And then I turned and stabbed at the radio contact on the console. The far funeral music died.

I stared at Quell and waited. An echo of the music lingered in the room.

"He still hears it," said Downs.

Suddenly, breaking the silence, a horn, a klaxon, a bell, and a voice: "Red alert! Crew to stations! Red alert!"

I turned and ran, following Downs along the corridor toward the main deck.

Reaching my post, I brought up the lights on the multi-level screen before me. A pattern of atomic light, many-colored, played before my eyes.

"What is that?" I wondered aloud.

Redleigh came to stand behind me, and posed the question, "Leviathan?"

The captain approached with his pulsing electric sound.

"No. The great comet's beyond, still some distance away. It sends a messenger ahead to warn us off. It fires a storm of gravities, atomic whirlwinds, dust storms of meteors, cosmic bombardments, solar explosions. Pay it no mind. That is but a mere mote of dust compared to Leviathan."

I tuned into the sensors on my console, and it was as the captain said. Somewhere, nearly out of range, far off but approaching fast, was a behemoth of unimaginable size and power.

Our spacecraft trembled.

Chapter 9

The trembling became more convulsive, the light on the screen more erratic. The sound grew loud, but, we knew, it was not the immense sound Leviathan might make when it arrived.

"Captain," said Redleigh. "Permission to turn back. We'll be destroyed."

"Head on, Mr. Redleigh," said the captain. "It's merely testing us."

The storm on the screen rose and fell and rose again. And then, a sudden silence.

"What?" said Redleigh.

The captain said, "What, what, indeed!"

"It's gone," I said, checking my screen again in disbelief. "The storm that ran before the comet is gone. But what of Leviathan itself?"

I ran some more scans, searching the vast expanse around our ship for hostile entities. "The comet! It's vanished, too! It's gone from the sensors."

"No!" said the captain.

"Yes," I said. "According to the readings, all the space around us is empty."

"Thank God," said Redleigh, almost to himself.

"No, I say, no!" the captain yelled. "My eyes see nothing. Yet—it *must* be there. I can almost touch it. I *feel* it. It is—"

A familiar voice broke in. "Gone," Quell said, quietly, staring at the emptiness of space on the computer screen. "Gone."

"Quell!" I cried. "You've come back! Thank God."

Quell said nothing.

"Quell, what happened," I asked. "Out there?"

Quell moved forward slowly. "The funeral music—it's gone. Our traveling burial grounds, gone. The comet, the nightmare, all . . . gone."

"Yes," I said. "But why?"

Quell remained silent.

"Out with it, man!!" cried the captain.

Quell finally turned away from the screen and spoke to us. "That storm has wounded Time. We have turned a corner in Eternity. The very stuff of the void, the abyss has been . . . turned wrong side out . . . atom on atom . . . molecule on molecule . . . particle on particle reversed . . . I feel it . . . *so.*"

And Quell reached out a hand as if his mind had fled.

"It can't be!" I heard myself say.

"So say I!" said the captain, disbelieving.

"Space says otherwise," said Quell, calmly. "The storm has picked us up and thrown us back two thousand years. The past has become our present."

"If this is now the past," said Redleigh, "what year is it?"

Quell thought for a few moments. "Before Columbus? Yes, certainly. Before the birth of Christ? Most likely. Before your Caesar built his Roman roads through Britain's moors, or Plato spoke or Aristotle listened? Maybe. That great star, the beast, it pities us."

"Pity?" said the captain. "How can you say pity?"

Quell searched through space with eye and mind. "It would not fight with us. Instead, it would hide us deep, so it would not be forced to war against us. It has given us a chance, a path away from it. *That,* sir, is pity."

"I will have none!" the captain said.

"Elijah," I whispered.

"What?" the captain turned toward my voice.

"Elijah. The day before our liftoff from Earth. Elijah said—"

"Said *what*?" the captain demanded impatiently.

"'Far out in space, there'll come a time when you see land where there is no land, find time where there is no time; when ancient kings will reflesh their bones and reseat their crowns . . .'"

"Is that time now?" asked Redleigh.

And Quell replied, "Yes, now. For look. And . . . *feel*."

I finished the memory of Elijah's words: "'Then, oh then, ship, ship's captain, ship's men, all, all will be destroyed! All save *one*.'"

All save one, I thought, as the captain exploded with rage. "Fools, damn fools!" he cried. "We do not take this past, accept these ancient years. We do not hide in pyramids or run from locust plagues to cower, grovel underneath the robes of Christ! We will stand forth."

He turned and strode toward the lift to the upper reaches. "The airlock, open it! Although blind, I will go forth and find the monster myself!"

Chapter 10

Quell's mind moved outside the ship to find the captain, alone.

And though I could not see, I heard, and what the captain finally said was this: "What? Nothing? All quiet, gone, spent? Is this the end? No more the hunt, the journey, and the goal? That terrifies me most: No more the goal! From here on then, what is the captain for? What does he do, if time and circumstance knock all the mountains down to one dull flat and endless plain, one long bleak winter afternoon, not even tea and simple bread to brighten it?

"Oh Christ, the thought of mindless noons that have no ends, or end in maunderings, stale tea leaves in a cup which tell no murders and no blood, and so no life—*that* breaks my bones. The sound of one leaf turning in a book would crack my spine. One dust mote burning on a sunlit hearth would smother my soul. The simple things that snug themselves in halls too clean, too quiet, that lie in well-made beds and smile idiot smiles! Oh, turn away. Such peace is a winepress to crush your soul.

"And yet . . . God, *feel* . . . the universe itself fills me this hour with quiet joy. Unseen by me, there one small fire goes out, but yet another freshens itself forth in birth. It is my heart's midnight, but yet some foundling sun reminds me that somewhere a million light-years on, a boy gets out of bed in cold well-water morn; the circus now arrives, a life's begun with animals and flags and bunting and bright lights. Would I deny his right, his joy at rising to run forth and greet the show? I would deny, I *would*!

"But no, ah God, but surely no. It cracks my heart to think of him derelict with age, but would I warn him not to turn the page and let life begin?

"I would! Our very life's a sin against itself!

"But then again, once more, I'd keep my tongue and let him play. Go, boy, I would advise, on some far world. Start up the day, spin forth your captured joys. O, know delight. Mind not on me. I stay here with my night."

Suddenly Small was behind me, and reached over my shoulder to adjust some controls on the console. The screen came to life, and we saw the captain out on the hull, tethered to the ship by an airline. Redleigh, similarly suited for space and tied to the ship by a line, hovered a few yards behind the captain. He had a weapon in his hand, but indecision showed on his face behind his airmask. Quell's mind moved, searching, and he touched good Redleigh's mind and in his thoughts I read: "When he speaks so, what must I do? Destroy or not destroy? And even as he moves back and forth, from light to dark, his madness most inconstant, so my own sanity wavers. I would kill him. But then again, I would not."

"Leviathan!" yelled the captain at the black emptiness surrounding him. "Stand forth! You *must* be there!"

I heard his breath rasping in the silent void, as he waited for an answer that would not come.

"Oh, God," he continued. "Give me, oh give me back just one millionth part of all the visions of my youth. Restore my sight. For just one moment in this long night, give me the strength that vision gives to finish out this thing, see darkness with these eyes, know whiteness then for death, do justice with these hands! Give back, oh I beseech, I humbly ask, I do cry out, I *pray*!"

At this the captain spun around, as if he was about to fall in the zero gravity of space, as if the weight of all he had said was too much.

"Captain!" Redleigh cried out. "No!"

"But yes . . . it's *given.*" The captain struggled to right himself. "Hold on, it's given back! My vision is clear. The universe stands right. I can see! The stars! My God, the billion stars, the stars!"

At which the captain wept.

Redleigh, seeing those same stars, spoke to himself. "Oh thank you, God, for miracles which teach. But then, I wonder, will he *learn*?"

"Who is that?" the captain said. "Redleigh? Is that you? My *friend's* face seen at last?"

He reached out and almost touched the faceplate of his first mate's helmet.

Redleigh responded, "It is the face of a friend. And this friend says, Turn back. There is still time. Time comes back to us. Your sight is healed. What more can you ask for now? It is a sign, a miracle. It is a true gift given you, sir. Now *act* on it."

"I will," the captain said. "Let me drink first. Let me look. Oh, Redleigh, it is like fresh mountain water. It is a cold, clear thing, this gift of seeing once again. Oh, God, the universe is lovely strange. I have hungered for it for thirty years. There is no bottom to my thirst. Let me stare. Let me truly stand alert. Let my eyes open wide, there, and yet more and more."

There was a soft pulsation of green and yellow light on the monitor before us, a far sound of bells and cries of murmuring waves and crowds.

I listened, close.

"Quell," I asked. "What is it?"

"Time," Quell said, "turns upon itself."

"Look, and *feel*!" the captain said.

And Quell told all that he felt and saw: "The knot falls loose . . . great Time unties itself. The years reverse. We have returned. Leviathan gives back our time and years. This is 2099."

"2099," the captain said. "Redleigh, did you hear?"

"Yes, Captain, yes!"

"We are once again in our proper hour! Two gifts, Mr. Redleigh. The gift of seeing and the gift of long-returning years."

"God is generous, Captain. He has corrected the calendar and touched your eyes."

"Would that *that* were true."

"It *is*!"

"No, it only *seems* to be so," the captain said. "Not God but the beast has made these offerings. It bribes me to stand clear. It sweetens me with banquetings of sight to mend my soul and fend me off. That stuff is spoiled. Need be, I'll now sew up these eyes or pluck them out with these two hands. I do not bribe. I do not take. I do not stay. If time is given me, I'll use it to make plans. If sight is given me, I'll use it well to mark my enemy's burial place. Leviathan, thy gifts will be a sword into thy breast!"

"Captain, it says escape!"

"To what? To run to Earth and on the way have time reversed again so we are greeted by the bones of Charlemagne or fall dead with Caesar, bloodied in his forum?"

"Christ's bones! God's ghost, oh give me strength to pull this trigger."

The weapon Redleigh carried was now pointed directly at the captain.

"You never will."

"But if I could!" said Redleigh. "How fine to land back home and go with simple cavemen into a cave, live out a life less a nightmare than all this, lie down with saber-tooths, sweet Christ, and *rest* awhile."

"We shall rest, Mr. Redleigh, at the dead heart of the comet."

"I see," said Redleigh. "Now I *am* dead. Let me put away my gun. Here comes Leviathan, to pick my bones. Shall I greet it, Captain, with you?"

There was a great light, an immense sound, a fantastic approaching dazzle and splendor.

And Quell echoed, "To pick my bones."

Chapter 11

"Sir?"

Quell came to attention as Downs came on deck.

"Sir, your suit is finished." The engineer held out a suit made of some stiff black material.

"Much thanks," said Quell. "It is a fine piece of work."

Downs tapped on the metal carapace. "I am tempted to die and wear the damned thing myself."

"Stick around," said Quell. "You may get your wish."

"Quell!" I said.

Quell stiffened, alert, turning toward me.

"You heard it all."

"The captain," I said, "has been given his sight, but is more blind than ever before."

"And we shall share his blindness," said Quell. "Look!"

The dazzling storm of light grew behind my eyes, where Quell had placed it. Likewise, it burst on the screens all around the deck.

"All hands!" the captain commanded. "Emergency life-suits on! Ready and stand by emergency life-craft! Redleigh, *inside*! All hands! All hands!"

The crew ran with eager shouts.

"Oh, yes," I said to myself. "The comet approaches. And it *is* a great white holy terror that fills the universe and swallows every star. And look, my God, oh look! The crew! They run like children run at their games."

"Listen to their thoughts," Quell said, gesturing at the people rushing madly around us. "I give you leave. The hot blood rushes in their veins. Hear how they *truly* run!"

He touched my brow and their thoughts flowed into mine. I felt and heard the shriek, the joyous cry, the glorious wail and shout of men running downhill to doom.

The captain appeared among us, and all hands turned to him, faces flushed with anticipation.

"Have you ever seen the like?!" said the captain. "Oh God, that fire, brighter than ten million suns. Everyone to stations."

"Aye aye, sir!" the crew shouted as one.

"Now," said the captain by radio to the crew in their suits, "in each and every life-craft ship, know the engines of destruction. Draw on my hunger to devour this thing—make it yours! In each craft is a beam more powerful than any hell-fire laser ever built. Wider, longer, swifter, surer. Use that power! Fret the beast. Lay him waste. Life-craft One under command of crewman Downs?"

"Downs here," cried the man. "Life-craft One ready!"

"Launch!"

I heard the first craft blast away, carrying Downs and his companion.

"Life-craft Two!" the captain shouted. "Crewman Small!"

"Small here," a voice replied. "Life-craft Two . . . ready!"

"Launch!"

Concussion, and Small and his voice and his crewmate were gone.

"Mr. Redleigh," said the captain, turning to his first mate. "The third craft is yours. Use it well."

"Sir!" said Redleigh.

"Quell," said the captain. And I saw that Quell had donned his black suit. "Quell, you go with Redleigh.

Ishmael stays with me, here on the main ship. Stand by for launch of Life-craft Three."

"Quell," Redleigh said, as the two prepared to leave the main deck. "You wear your suit of death."

"It fits, Mr. Redleigh, it fits."

"Will there be room for me?"

"Death," Quell said, "makes a large coffin. We shall not knock elbows."

"All right," said Redleigh. "Then, on the double."

Quell turned to me before leaving, as if to say something.

"Quell," I said, "let me go with you. Captain? I must ask—"

But Quell cut in. "No. Stay. And live. You *will* live, you know, to be very old. I, who sees beyond, tell you this. Be old, Ishmael. Be happy. Dear friend, goodbye."

"Oh, Quell," I whispered. "Leave your mind with me, so we may be friends to the end."

I felt his thoughts, his mind did linger in my ears and in my head.

"My mind is yours," said Quell as he left. "Yours."

A few moments later, the captain commanded, "Launch Life-craft Three!"

Redleigh's voice came over the intercom, "Life-craft Three launching!"

Concussion. Quell and Redleigh catapulted into the universe.

“Ishmael, stand close,” said the captain.

“Sir!” I said.

“They fly,” the captain said. “There, see the life-crafts as they go.”

Watching the computer screen, we saw the craft, already far out beyond us, and heard their voices, mingled. And in those lonely craft, Quell, Redleigh, Small, and Downs. The voices said, “Craft One, full speed. Craft Two, full. Three, on target.”

“Oh, Ishmael, look!” the captain said. “That is the whole Antarctic continent, all white, and somehow hurled upon the universal air to shake our sight! Leviathan!”

“It’s too much!” I cried. “I cannot see!”

“Let it burn your eyes, as it burned mine,” the captain said. “We’ll still have hands to put it out!”

“Quell!” I shouted.

For I was hearing music: the music of Quell’s ancestors, the funeral dirge of his grandfather. It was in Quell’s mind, and somehow it came to me.

Quell’s voice replied, long miles away: “I hear you, young friend.”

“Oh, Quell, that music!”

“Yes,” Quell said. “Leviathan has learned that tune . . . and plays it well.”

And then the music was playing not only in my head, but coming over the ship's speakers—loud, crashing, melancholy waves.

Suddenly the captain said, "I'll stop that sound! I'll kill that thing! Crafts One and Two—destroy! Craft Three—destroy! Redleigh—destroy!"

And Redleigh's voice, in concert with the others, echoed back: "Destroy!"

The music crescendoed—immense sounds and vibrations. It swelled and rose and fell away.

"Destroy and be destroyed," I said to myself, remembering. To the captain, I said, "Oh, sir, our ships are too small. That comet destroys *them*! I see the men's bones, as if on an X-ray. The laser-beam weapons they aim are no more than matchstick torches against that great hand of fire that closes in on them like a fist."

I watched as Life-crafts One, Two, and Three disappeared.

"There," I whispered. "I faintly see. My vision fades. The ships, one by one, fall, plucked free of skins, their metal skeletons revealed, the men tossed out in millrace radiation. Flashing meteors . . . all swallowed . . . vanishing."

"No, good Ishmael," came Quell's faint whisper. "We are gone, but we have each been thrown to a different warp in Time."

"The men in Life-craft One," I asked, "their weapons stilled, where do they go?"

Quell's whisper said, "Our friend Downs is sent to death, perhaps, and burial with Richard, mad lost king, on his green plain, his crown and blood tossed at his feet."

"The men in Life-craft Two spin further on. They drop, despairing, where?"

"In Illinois. Oh strange," came Quell's mute words.

"In Illinois, near the tomb where Lincoln sleeps. And Redleigh? Quell, what of him?"

"Still here. We know not where we go. This comet steers us. *Time* is its weapon!"

I turned to the captain. "Time," I said. "The comet has flung them throughout Time. Quell says Time is its weapon."

"As Time is mine!" said the captain. "My crew dispersed, my weapons gone, yet I have one huge weapon left, aboard this ship. Time! Time is all! So I have made an engine that, like Leviathan, can twist all Time like a spinning top. Now, with my vast machine we'll use the comet's power against itself. As in the Orient, we fall and take our killer with us, using all his weight for his defeat. That mouth which would have swallowed us, we will cause to gape and turn about. What's larger than Leviathan? Eternity! The void! The dark abyss! The stuff *between* the stars! That is the mouth *I* use. My engine will open a seam in space and drop Leviathan in."

And in that instant, our captain played some keys of the main computer console and the engines of our rocket throbbed to hysteria.

"Leviathan," cried the captain, "meet Leviathan! Destruction, meet destruction! Comet, see thy mirror image! Annihilation, *know* annihilation!"

The entire universe around us shook. I heard Quell's voice as it faded among the stars.

"Oh, Ishmael."

"Quell!"

The captain's voice was loud in that last great sound, and in that final moment he shouted, "What? My ship gone, too? Its flesh ripped free? Its bones strewn forth? Am I blind once more? Then blind, I seize on thee! Dead, I grapple with thee. Where is thy heart? Oh there, now there—I'll stifle it. Oh damned and dread Leviathan, it comes to *this*!"

There was a final explosion—a great outpouring of shrapneled ship, lost humans, and wild beams. And I, thrown upward, floated in my life-suit above the wreckage, surrounded by mirages, dreams, motes, shadows, stars.

Gone, yes, all gone, I thought. Down the long black mineshaft of the universe, its bridal veil trailing despairs and woes, celebrating itself, a mindless mystery forever in motion, but . . . wait . . . now truly gone? Gone all the ships, men, large, small, sane or mad, the captain with them, madness maddened. Did he open wide the seam, that strange vast hole in eternity he spoke of, and drop Leviathan in? And are they lost forever? Or will, I wonder, Leviathan return? Will he return in thirty years and bring with him all those who would have killed him?

Long years from now, will the monster and my mates slide down the length of the abyss, return as one at last . . . the hunter and the hunted, the feared and the fearer, the madness and the vaulting dream of madness, together fused forever through centuries yet unborn? Will it all be here, will it all pass by when Earth is old and looks up to behold Leviathan, our ships, our crew, our captain—an endless cortege to the specter ghost?

A dark shape floated nearby, turning slowly. I recognized it as Quell's funeral suit.

"Quell!"

I reached out and seized the suit, and turning it, found it empty. I spoke to empty space. "No, just the chaff, the husk. My good friend gone. Oh, Quell."

I embraced the empty suit and the lost funeral music of Quell's ancestors sounded once again in my ears.

Alone, I floated with the memory of good Quell, who had gone to be with comets and their gods. I drifted so, aimlessly, holding on to the suit, a strange life-raft, knowing the air in my life-suit would soon be gone. How long? I wondered. A day, maybe two . . . until . . .?

Above, I see a light, and hear a voice through static.

"Starship *Rachel,* this is starship *Rachel* . . ."

A ship, passing, investigating the wreckage, comes to pick me up at last. The *Rachel,* who, in her long search for her missing children finds but another orphan. I let the coffin go. I let the memory of Quell go to his light-year burial ground.

The drama's done. Only one remains. I, Ishmael, alone, am here to tell you this.

"Starship *Rachel* standing by. We see you. Come aboard. Come aboard."